The Four Hoods
and Great Dog

The Four Hoods and Great Dog

Susan Fromberg Schaeffer

Illustrations by Norman Nodell

ST. MARTIN'S PRESS

New York

THE FOUR HOODS AND GREAT DOG. Copyright © 1988 by Susan Fromberg
Schaeffer. Illustrations by Norman Nodell. All rights reserved. Printed in the United
States of America. No part of this book may be used or reproduced in any manner
whatsoever without written permission except in the case of brief quotations embod-
ied in critical articles or reviews. For information, address St. Martin's Press, 175
Fifth Avenue, New York, N.Y. 10010.

Design by Claire Counihan

Library of Congress Cataloging-in-Publication Data

Schaeffer, Susan Fromberg.
  The four Hoods and Great Dog / by Susan Fromberg Schaeffer.
    p. cm.
  Summary: A move to the country introduces Steven and June Hood
to the kitten Foudini and the largest dog anybody has ever seen, two
talking animals who are preparing a return visit to the world from
which they originally came and decide to take the children with
them.
  ISBN 0-312-01431-7 : $12.95
  [1. Dogs—Fiction. 2. Cats—Fiction. 3. Fantasy.] I. Title.
PZ7.S3324Fo 1988
[Fic]—dc19   87-27476
                                                        CIP
                                                         AC

First Edition

10 9 8 7 6 5 4 3 2 1

for Benjamin and May

Contents

List of Illustrations

The Four Hoods
and Great Dog

Chapter 1

Moving to the Country

The four Hoods lived in the city, but they were not happy there. They knew other people who looked up at the Manhattan skyline and said how beautiful it was. They knew other people who did not mind looking up and seeing small, picture-puzzle pieces of sky fitted neatly between tall buildings. When the four Hoods looked down a city street, they liked to imagine the buildings rising in the air like gray mists, becoming thinner and thinner as they rose, until finally they were only gray clouds and were blown off by the wind. In place of the buildings, the four Hoods saw long, green meadows. But above all, the four Hoods saw animals.

The four Hoods were a family, a mother and father, a son named Steven, and a daughter named June. Steven and June's parents said that the city was not a good place for animals, but if they ever moved, they could have a dog. Perhaps they could even have a horse. Every September before school began, the children began their campaign for a dog. If they had a dog, they would walk it before they did their homework. They would sit up with it at night when it was sick. They would watch it carefully so that it never ran into the street and was hit by a car. "If we ever move to the country, then you can have a dog," said their parents. But every year when September came, they were enrolled in the local school, their parents went back to work, and the little Hoods gave up hope: they would never move.

Then, one morning, Mrs. Hood got up early and found the back door to their house wide open. That's odd, she thought. I'm sure I didn't leave the door open before I went to bed. She was still half-asleep. She rubbed her eyes and saw an electric cord snaking its way out beneath the living room door. A robbery! When she went into the living room, all the lamps were gone. "It is time to move to the country," said Mrs. Hood. If they stayed in the city, they would have to install an alarm system. There would be silver tapes on all their windows, and soon it would take them half an hour to get into the house.

Mrs. Hood earned a living finding mistakes in books about to be printed. "If God had wanted me to stay here and read," she reasoned, "he would not have let the thief steal all of our lights."

Mr. Hood, who wrote books, decided he could write books anywhere. The two small Hoods were asked if they wanted to move. "Can we have a dog if we move?" they asked. Yes, said their parents, they could. "Then we want to move," they said. "But how will we find a house?"

"I will find one this weekend," said Mr. Hood, and he drove to the country and found one. When he came back, he told his children that they would like the house because each of them would have their own bedroom. There was a stream in front of the house deep enough for swimming, and in the summer, when the leaves were on the trees, you couldn't see another house from the windows. "And," he said, "the house comes with a lot of land."

"How much?" asked Steven, the oldest of the children.

"About a city block," said his father.

"A city block!" said June Hood. "Everything is bigger in the country!"

"Even the sun looks bigger," said their mother. "Especially when it sets."

"When it sets, it looks like a tunnel," said June. "You can walk through to the other side."

"What's on the other side?" asked Steven.

"A city with buildings whose walls you can walk through. The buildings move from place to place like a herd of animals. They graze in the meadows, and then they move on to another field. It's a city but it's not a city."

"I'm not going through that tunnel," said Steven.

"June is making it up," said Mrs. Hood.

"No, I'm not," June said. "I dream about it. Everything is bigger on the other side. People are big as trees, and dogs are larger than horses. On the other side, we would be dwarfs."

"Dwarf! Dwarf!" said Steven, pointing at her. "You're a dwarf now!"

They chased each other out of the room while their mother called after them, "Stop fighting! Stop fighting!"

The Hoods were an odd family. In the first place, their real name was not Hood. Their real name was Brown. The people on the block had nicknamed them the four Hoods because they always wore parkas with pointed hoods. One day, as they were coming home from a drive in the country, one of the neighborhood children saw them getting out of their car and said, "Here come the four Hoods." The name stuck. The four Hoods liked their new name better than their old one. In school, when the children had to fill out forms, or write their

3

names on their papers, they would neatly print their true names: Brown. But when they moved to the country, they said, they would take their *true* name: Hood. All in all, they could not wait to go.

So when the truck came, and everything was wrapped in dull brown quilted cloths, they spent little time looking back. Before she left the house in the city, June looked over her shoulder and said that the rooms had grown bigger now that the furniture was gone. Mrs. Hood looked around, brushed the tears from her eyes, and got into the front seat. "No fighting in the back," she said.

"At least we won't have to make this trip every weekend," said her husband. "Now we'll be there all the time."

"Now you'll have to explain to everyone why you're named June," said her mother. "All over again." June sighed. Everyone thought she was named June because that was the month in which she had been born. But she had been born in May. She was named June after her grandmother.

"I don't care," said June. "Now we can have a dog."

"Not until we unpack and clean up the house," her mother said.

"I bet it's a terrible place," said Steven. "I bet the rocks in the stream are sharp and cut your feet. I bet the bedrooms are filled with spiders."

"Yuk!" shouted June, who was terrified of spiders.

"Keep quiet," said their mother.

"Or there'll be no dog," said their father.

The sun set, growing larger as it came to rest on the horizon. A small round moon had already risen in the still-light sky. The children fell asleep.

"I wonder what it will be like," said Mrs. Hood.

"It will be fine," said her husband. "It's what we always wanted to do."

4

Chapter 2

Finding Great Dog

It was dark when they arrived at the country house, but they could see the house plainly. It was a square white house with black shutters and a pointed roof, exactly the sort of house children draw when they first put pencil to paper. Mrs. Hood thought about those drawings, and remembered how, when her children began to draw, they always drew people who were tall enough to lean their elbows on the roof.

The moon was white and round and the house cut a sharp-edged shadow on the lawn in front of her. She would not be surprised to learn that June was right, and that if you walked into the doorway of the sun or the moon, you would find huge creatures on the other side. The country had always been a magic place for her.

She and her husband woke the children. Inside the house, they lay down on the floor, crawled into their sleeping bags, and went back to sleep. Mr. and Mrs. Hood sat in the half-furnished living room and said how happy they were to be there. Then they heard June crying. "I'm afraid," she said. She was used to hearing cars going by, honking, and motorcycles, and people talking on the street. Mrs. Hood said that if you listened carefully, you heard country noises. There were just as many of them. June cried on.

"In a few days," said her mother, "you won't miss the noises anymore."

"Did you hear something barking?" June asked her.

"No," said her mother. "Nothing barking."

"Not really barking," said June. "More like whining."

Her mother, who heard nothing, asked her what she thought it was. "A puppy," June said sleepily. "A puppy who walked through the sun from the other side because he knew we were coming."

"Go to sleep," her mother said. "Tomorrow is a busy day. We have to clean up the house and sign you kids up at school."

"School," said June, disgusted. "They have school even in the country!"

"Go to sleep," said her mother.

"I hear it barking," June said.

"You can look for it in the morning," said Mrs. Hood.

"Maybe it's a barking spider," said Steven, who had been lying awake, listening.

"Shut up!" said June.

The next day, Mr. and Mrs. Hood and some friends who drove up from the city to help them, swept out all the rooms and put away all the furniture. It was, after all, a big house. A door in the far wall of the kitchen led to a staircase and two bedrooms above the garage. These would be the studies, said Mr. and Mrs. Hood. Of course, they first needed fixing up. One room was in particularly disastrous shape: great chunks of plaster had fallen from the walls and in places the lathing showed clearly. Huge patches of flowered wallpaper peeled from the walls and hung there like monstrous petals. When the children began complaining that they didn't have enough to do, Mr. and Mrs. Hood told them to start peeling the wallpaper.

"Spiders!" said June.

"Dust!" said Steven.

"Get going," said their father.

The children began peeling off the wallpaper, comparing the strips they peeled from the walls to see whose was the largest.

"Look in here!" said June. "A little shoe! And a book! And a little red dress!"

"Look at this!" said Steven. "It looks like a skull! An animal must have crawled in here and gotten trapped." June came over and looked. She made a face, took a strip of wallpaper, and covered up the animal skull. "This is an *old* house," said Steven. "Mom has pictures of the stage coach that used to stop in front of it. Maybe it's *too* old."

"Did you hear that?" asked June. They both stood still. There it was again, the whimpering she had heard the night before.

"It's an animal trapped in the walls," said Steven. "Let's find him!"

The two children began stripping the paper from the walls, faster and faster, but still they couldn't find the whimpering animal. Finally, there was only one strip of wallpaper left. June took one edge and Steven the other, and they yanked. The whole piece came loose and fell to the floor. In back of it, cowering, was a puppy. He was brown and white and gray and tan. The tip of his nose was black, as was the tip of his tail, and he was looking up at the children happily, as if he were smiling.

"A puppy!" said June. She got down on her knees and crept toward him. He began wagging his little tail and, lying on his little round belly, inched toward her. "Come

7

He was looking up at the children happily.

on, little doggy," she said. The puppy inched further forward.

"Grab him!" said Steven.

June turned and glared at Steven. "And frighten him to death?" she asked. "Come on, little doggy, come on," she crooned. The dog moved forward. June grabbed him. He seemed perfectly happy in her arms. He looked up at her and began licking her chin. She giggled. The dog licked her cheek.

"Come on," said Steven. "It's my turn. Let him lick me."

They sat down on the floor and began petting the dog. He flipped over on his back. "He wants to be carried," said Steven, who picked him up. "I bet he's hungry."

The two children fell silent. It was too soon to tell their parents about the puppy. They were still cleaning up the house. And *they* hadn't even signed up for school yet. "Maybe we should sneak down for some food and bring it up," said Steven. June nodded. But what should they bring the puppy to eat? "The steak left over from lunch," Steven said.

"Where are you going with that steak?" his mother asked just as Steven was about to start back up the stairs.

"I was hungry," said Steven.

"You should have eaten your lunch," said his mother, but, as she started back to the living room, she stopped and listened. "What was that noise?" she asked.

Stephen said he didn't hear any noise.

"It wasn't *any* noise," said his mother. "It sounded like a bark."

"Probably just June doing an animal imitation," he said.

His mother said she would just come up and see how they were doing with the wallpaper. "Not *now*," said

Steven. "Wait until we're finished. We want to surprise you."

"Upstairs," said his mother.

June was sitting in the middle of the room, on top of a pile of stiff, peeled wallpaper, the dog in her lap. "Don't blame me, Ma," she said, looking up. "He came out of the *wall*."

"Out of the what?" asked Mrs. Hood.

"The *wall*," said June, and explained how they found the dog. She reminded her mother that she'd promised them a dog as soon as they moved to the country, and this one came with the house. In fact, he came wrapped *in* the house. Didn't she like him? He was only a baby. She stood up and walked over to her mother, carrying the puppy.

"He's cute," said her mother, "but . . ." Just then the puppy leaned forward and kissed Mrs. Hood on the cheek. "Do you promise to walk him?" Mrs. Hood asked. Her children promised. "Every day, no matter what the weather?"

"Even in earthquakes," said Steven.

"There are no earthquakes around here," said his mother. "What about in sun and storm and wind and rain and snow? Do you promise?"

They promised. They swore. They crossed their hearts.

"But," said their mother, "he's awfully large for a puppy. He's the size of a shoebox already."

"He's not so big," said June.

"If you ask me," said their mother, "he looks bigger than he did when I first came into the room."

"Look at the size of those paws," said their father later. "He's going to be as big as a horse."

"He's larger than he was when I saw him upstairs," said their mother. "Isn't he larger?"

"I don't think so," said June. But he *was* larger. He

10

was heavier and harder to pick up, and they had found him only three hours ago. Before June went to bed, she went into Steven's room. "Do you think he's growing already?" she asked.

"I don't know," said her brother.

The puppy rested his head on the edge of Steven's mattress.

"What's he standing on?" Steven asked.

"On the *floor*," said June. "He's going to be big as a house."

"What do you think we should call him?" Steven asked.

"I think we should call him Great Dog," said June. "I mean, look how big he is, and he's only a puppy. He can't get much bigger, can he?"

From the doorway, their mother said, "I certainly hope not."

By the end of the week, Great Dog had grown so large that it was no longer possible to keep him in the house. He was a sweet and intelligent dog, and saw how upset everyone became when he knocked something over, like a couch or a china cabinet, and took to walking slowly and quietly through the rooms. But by the end of the week, the tips of his ears touched the ceiling, and everyone agreed something had to be done.

"We'll keep him in the barn," said June and Steven.

"I think we should send him to the zoo," said Mr. Hood. The two children burst into tears.

"What a thing to say," said Mrs. Hood, who had been thinking the very same thing. "No, we'll put him in the barn. We'll have to find out how to heat it during the winter."

"Cleaning out the barn will take weeks," said their father. But it did not take very long. If a huge log needed to be hauled out, the children would say, "Get the log, get the log," and Great Dog would carry it out in his teeth. The barn was getting cleaner and emptier and they had barely begun. Then Great Dog started barking.

"What does he want?" asked Steven.

June watched Great Dog, who was dancing around a huge log he had dropped in the middle of the lawn.

"I think," she said, "he wants us to throw it for him."

"Throw it for him!" said Steven. "I can't even pick it up!"

"Maybe if we gave it a push and started rolling it down the hill," said June. When they pushed the log, Great Dog jumped into the air, and chased the log until he caught it. Then he carried it back to them in his teeth, dropped it at their feet, and began wagging his tail.

"This isn't going to be as simple as we thought," said Steven.

"Not simple at all," said June.

"But he doesn't wake us up in the morning like our friend Allison's dog does," said Steven, "because he sleeps in the barn. So we get some peace and quiet."

The next morning, June awoke to the sound of something bumping heavily against her windowpane: thud, thud, thud. Birds, she thought. Go away. *Thud, thud, thud.* The noise was getting louder. My window is going to break, thought June. She sat up in bed and looked at the window. There was Great Dog, standing on his hind legs, patting her windowpane with his enormous front paw.

"Woof!" said Great Dog.

"Go back to sleep," June told him.

"WOOF!" said Great Dog.

"I'm coming, I'm coming," said June. She went downstairs, and out to the barn, where she filled his breakfast bowl. She couldn't understand why, but large as he was, he didn't eat more than an ordinary dog. "It's a good

12

thing you don't have a big appetite," she told Great Dog, "or we couldn't afford to keep you."

"Woof," said Great Dog agreeably, as if to say he'd already thought of that.

"Are you going to get even larger?" June asked him. "The tips of your ears already come up to the top of the first-floor window panes. You can't get any larger, can you?" she asked.

"Woof," said Great Dog. June had the dreadful feeling he meant to say yes, he *could* grow larger, and he *would* grow larger.

Chapter 3

The School Bus Fiasco

Suffice it to say that Great Dog grew and grew until, when he stood on all four legs, his ears were as high as the weathervane on the roof of the house. At first, people came from all over to look at him, but everyone soon became used to him. When the Hood children arrived at school in the morning, the first thing everyone would ask them was, "What has Great Dog done now?"

He had always done *something*. Because he was so tall, the four Hoods walked between his legs and beneath his stomach. Once or twice, Great Dog forgot people were likely to be walking under him and almost lay down upon them. "It was like a bridge falling on you," Steven told his friend.

"It was like a *mountain* falling on you," June told her friend.

"How do you pet him?" the children asked.

"Oh, he lies down," said June.

"We hold onto his fur and climb up on him," said Steven.

"If he needs a combing, we use a rake. We have to use a rake when he wants his belly scratched. Otherwise it would take us all morning."

"Does he chase cats?" asked one of the children.

14

"No, he likes cats," said June. "They run up his nose and slide down his side. Sometimes they sit between his ears. He likes chasing bears, but we have to go up to the big mountains and we usually don't have time to take him. But Steven's getting stonger. He throws the small logs for him. He'd rather play with the cats. He lets them walk right into his mouth. You should have seen one of the cats. He disappeared right into Great Dog's mouth. Only his legs were sticking out. But Great Dog learns fast. He never lets cats walk far down his tongue anymore. He comes when he's called, and he's stopped sitting in the middle of the road."

One day Great Dog decided to sit in the middle of the road and caused the first traffic jam ever seen in that part of the country. He sat on the white line in the middle of the road, and no matter what people said to him, or how loudly they honked their horns, he refused to move. After an hour, a milk truck, a grocery truck, a mail truck, a school bus, and fifteen cars were lined up in one direction. In the other direction was a fire engine that tried showering Great Dog with water, hoping to convince him to leave the road, and behind the fire engine was a very long line of cars indeed. Every time a horn blared, Great Dog would tilt his head, first to the right, then to the left, as if to say, what an interesting noise. He stayed there until the four Hoods came back from shopping in Greenfield and found him.

"You bad dog," said June. "No peanut butter sandwiches for you today." (June always took peanut butter sandwiches in her lunchbox, but she never ate them. Usually, one of her friends had something more interesting to eat, and she would persuade one of them to share lunch with her. When she came home, she fed her sandwiches to Great Dog.) Great Dog's ears went down, his tail slid between his legs, and he slowly got up and slunk after June. The cars began moving along the road. The police chief came to the house and warned the four Hoods that if Great Dog continued to sit in the middle of the road, they would have to do something about him.

"He won't do it again," said Steven. "He never makes the same mistake twice."

"He's too interested in the road, if you ask me," said Mr. Hood.

"That's only because he's waiting for the school bus," said Steven. "He watches it take us away in the morning, and he waits for it to bring us back again at night."

"Tell the dog to watch from the meadow in front of our house," said Mr. Hood.

"Fred, don't be ridiculous," said Mrs. Hood. "The dog can't understand English."

"He can!" said Steven and June together. And they may have been right, because after that day, Great Dog waited for the bright yellow bus in the meadow in front of the house. During the day, he played with the huge bale of hay the farmers had made into an enormous ball for him. At other times, he rolled heavy logs up and down the hill in front of the house. Occasionally, he disappeared into the woods and came out with his ears drooping, so that everyone knew he had seen something unusual, but no one knew what.

One day, the school bus came merrily along the curve in the road and Great Dog watched it happily. Soon Steven and June would get off, June would feed him her peanut butter sandwiches, and she and Steven would comb his stomach with the rake while he lay on his back shaking his paws at the sky. Then he would show them the tunnel he had dug under the snow. He had worked on it all morning and it now ran all around the house.

Suddenly, the school bus stopped and didn't move. He watched, waiting for the school bus to choke into life and move down the road toward him. Instead, he heard the children inside shouting, waving and pointing. He turned his head and there was a huge black bear. The bear had also seen the bus stop and had come up to it and was now shaking it with one paw and clawing at a window with another.

This will not do at all, thought Great Dog, and he bounded across the creek to the school bus. "Great Dog will save us!" shouted the children. Steven and June looked at one another. Great Dog would certainly drive off the bear, but who knew what he would do next? He was only six months old, still a puppy.

Great Dog came up quietly behind the bear. "WOOF!" he said. The bear turned around, saw him, and got down on all fours and galloped back into the woods. Great Dog looked at the bus and saw it still was not moving. It wasn't a very safe place, he decided, not if there were bears who came out of the woods from the side of the road, not if there were fire engines that turned their hoses on anything that stopped near the white line. So he picked up the school bus as if it were a yellow log, and with the bus in his mouth, he walked off the road, into the river, and began to swim to the other side.

"Oh, my God!" the children screamed. The bus driver had turned white and held onto the wheel, staring straight ahead. "He's going to drown us! He's going to drop us in the water!" the children cried. But Great Dog did no such thing. He trotted up and down the shore, looking for a nice, sandy place, and then lay the bus down. Then, with a pleased expression, he began trotting up and down, looking for Steven and June. When he saw them, his tail wagged so fast it knocked over several small saplings and four medium-sized pine trees.

"I think we can get out now," said Steven. The bus driver turned his head slightly. He seemed to have forgotten how to blink. "If you open the door," Steven said

He picked up the schoolbus as if it were a yellow log.

to the driver, "we can get out. Great Dog chased away the bear."

The bus driver pulled the lever to open the door, and the children climbed out. "Now what?" asked Allison.

"People will come for us with boats," said Danny, Steven's friend.

"But what about the *bus*?" asked the driver. "We can't leave the *bus* here."

"No," said Steven. "Great Dog," he said sternly, pointing at the bus, "what are we going to do about this?"

Great Dog wagged his tail. He lay down on the sand and flipped over, waiting to be congratulated for rescuing them and waiting for his stomach to be scratched. On the other side of the river, Mr. and Mrs. Hood were shouting and waving their arms. "Bring back the bus!" Mr. Hood was shouting to the dog. Great Dog lay happily on his back and waggled his great paws in the air.

"Great Dog," said June. "Sit up."

Great Dog sat up, his ears pointed. What game was she going to play now? He liked to see so many children. They could *all* scratch his stomach. He loved Steven and June, but he often wished Mr. and Mrs. Hood had wanted more children. Steven got tired of throwing logs for him. If there were more boys in the family, he would have more people to play with.

"Fetch the stick," said June, and threw a large branch for him. He caught it easily and looked reproachfully at her. Couldn't she think of something more interesting for him to do?

"Fetch the bus," said June.

Great Dog looked at her suspiciously. Fetch the bus? He knew perfectly well he was supposed to leave the bus alone. He had picked it up only to take it away from the bears. True, he had only seen one bear, but when there was one bear, there must be others. "Fetch the bus," said June, "and take it to Mother."

Take it to Mother? thought Great Dog. But Mother was shouting and waving her hands. Mother was angry at him. He was not taking the bus to Mother.

It was getting dark, and still Great Dog would not pick up the bus. More and more people were on the other side of the river, shouting at Great Dog and at Mr. and Mrs. Hood.

"We have to do something," said Steven.

"But what?" asked June.

"Let's get back on the bus," said Steven.

"What good will that do?" asked June.

"Come on, you pest," he said. "Don't ask so many questions."

"Shouldn't everyone get on the bus?" asked June.

"Get *on*," said Steven, who wished his parents had produced a raccoon instead of a younger sister.

"Well, now what?" asked June. "We're on the bus and it's getting dark and everyone's cold."

"Great Dog," said Steven. "Pick up the bus."

Great Dog looked at the children in the bus.

"Fetch the bus," said Steven.

Great Dog thought it over. The children never asked him to do anything that would get him in trouble. Slowly, carefully, he picked the bus up in his mouth.

"Bring the bus to Mother," Steven said. "She won't be mad at you." Great Dog looked sadly at him, as if to say, why are you playing such a mean trick on me? She will surely be mad at me and I won't have any supper or breakfast or stomach scratchings for a week.

"Bring the bus to Mother," said Steven. Great Dog got up and sadly walked into the river, the bus in his mouth. Then he began swimming to the other side.

"He looks like he has a big yellow pencil in his mouth," someone said to Mrs. Hood.

"I wonder what possessed him to swim off with a bus," said someone else. No one sounded very angry. Great Dog was climbing up the other side of the river bank, the bus in his teeth. He crossed the road and gently put the bus down in front of Mrs. Hood. Then he lay down with his head between his paws, looking up sadly.

Steven and June explained that the bus had stalled, and a bear had attacked it, and Great Dog had rescued them. Of course, said Steven, Great Dog had odd ideas about how to rescue people.

"I'll bake him the biggest dog biscuit anyone's ever seen," said the woman who lived in the house down the road.

"He may not be the most sensible dog in the world," said the woman's husband, "but his heart's in the right place."

"How are we going to get the other children back?" asked Mrs. Hood.

"Oh, that's easy," said June. "Great Dog," she said, "fetch the bus. Take it back." And Great Dog took the bus back across the river, waited until the children were seated inside, and then swam back to the other side. Then everyone came over to the Hoods for toasted marshmallows and hot chocolate, and the next day, the story of Great Dog's rescue was on the front page of *The Timboro Reformer*.

"I wonder if he'd fetch a garbage truck if we asked him to," Steven asked June.

"I heard that!" said Mr. Hood. "Don't ask him to fetch anything larger than a newspaper." Mr. Hood looked outside. It was snowing again. "Take Great Dog and dig out the driveway," he said. Great Dog loved to dig. When the Hoods first moved in, Great Dog dug huge holes and they had once driven their car into one of them. It was no trouble for Great Dog to dig out the driveway. He was cheaper than a snowplow, said Mr. Hood, even if he was more peculiar.

Chapter 4

The Roof Falls In

Great Dog was on his best behavior after rescuing the school bus. He was happy to be petted and told what a good dog he was, but he seemed to know that no matter how good people told him he'd been, they were still *nervous* about a dog who could, if he wanted to, pick up a school bus and swim with it in his teeth to the other side of the river. He helped Mrs. Hood carry logs from the shed to the front porch, and when there was a heavy snowfall, he would dig the car out of the drifts so that the four Hoods were always the first on the road. He seemed happy to lie about in the barn, on his back, and play with Foudini, the small black-and-white cat who had wandered up one day and decided to live in the barn with him.

At first everyone worried that Great Dog would accidentally hurt the small cat. He might roll over on him and crush him without intending to. But Foudini was a careful cat and something of a warrior: whenever Great Dog did something that displeased him, the cat would stand up on his hind legs, and whack Great Dog on the nose. Occasionally, when Great Dog was lying in the barn, thinking about whatever there was to think about that day, Foudini would come over and whack him on the nose on principle. In the end, the four Hoods found themselves scolding Foudini for bullying Great Dog, because Great Dog would never dream of hurting Foudini. If the cat went out into the meadow and cried, no matter how softly, Great Dog bounded after him, rushing to his rescue. For a while, the four Hoods thought Foudini was becoming spoiled and foolish. He would go up to a raccoon and threaten it, knowing perfectly well that all he had to do was squeak and Great Dog would bound to the rescue. "But what if Great Dog is asleep?" Steven asked June. "Or if the cat gets too far away and Great Dog can't hear him?"

They looked over at Great Dog, who was lying on the barn floor looking depressed. His pan of food had just been set out, and as usual, Foudini was picking out the pieces of liver and eating them first. "I never saw anything like it," said Mr. Hood. "Great Dog lets that cat bully him silly." Foudini gave Mr. Hood a nasty look and went on eating. When he was finished, he went into the dark corner of the barn, and came back with something brown in his mouth. It was a dead mouse. The cat looked at the Hoods to be sure they were all paying attention, and then dropped the mouse into the center of Great Dog's plate. Great Dog seemed happy to eat the mouse.

"Yuk!" said Steven and June together.

"The cat believes in sharing," said Mrs. Hood.

Great Dog swiped softly at the cat, washing him clean with one lick of his tongue. When he finished, the cat's fur stood up in points, as if he had been sprayed with mousse. "What a pair," said Mr. Hood.

"They're so quiet," said Mrs. Hood. "It's a pleasure to watch them."

"It won't last," said Mr. Hood. "It's been two weeks since the school bus, and there's no trouble. It's too good to be true."

Great Dog let the cat bully him silly.

The cat listened to him, yawned, showing his pink tongue, and curled up between Great Dog's paws.

"They look like they're planning something," said Mrs. Hood. Mr. Hood said not to be silly. Anyone knew animals couldn't plan.

After the four Hoods left, Foudini and Great Dog went outside. The *dog* walked outside; the cat rode on his back, his claws dug into the dog's fur. Foudini had his eye on a bird's nest. All winter, four birds flew back and forth to a nest just over Steven's window. Steven believed Foudini called the birds "the four flying feasts," and noticed that Foudini found them particularly irresistible after a heavy rain, when they appeared to be flying complete with sauce. Foudini had tried climbing up on the window frame inside the house. He had tried scaling the outside wall. He had climbed up on Great Dog and launched himself through the air at the nest, but always missed it and ended up back on the ground, bruised, his pride also black and blue. Great Dog was worried about Foudini's many falls and was becoming more and more reluctant to carry the cat over to the nest. He knew that if he simply pushed the nest from the wall of the house onto the ground, the cat would have his birds, but then Foudini would have nothing to do during the day. On top of that, Great Dog liked the birds and did not want Foudini to drop one of them into the middle of his lunch dish. He was standing under the nest wondering what to do, when Steven, who had been sent home from a friend's house because he had several suspicious-looking spots on his cheeks, crossed the bridge and came toward them.

Steven saw where Great Dog was standing and told Foudini to leave the birds alone. Foudini sighed with irritation. No one *ever* paid attention to him. He was too small. Soon Steven would start playing with Great Dog and he would be put in the house or the barn.

27

"Lie down," Steven told Great Dog, and when Great Dog did as he was told, Steven plucked Foudini from the dog's back, opened the side door, and put him in the kitchen.

Fine, thought Foudini. No birds and another boring day.

He sat in the window and watched Steven, who apparently intended to throw logs for Great Dog. Aren't they boring? thought Foudini. The same thing, day after day.

But today Steven had plans for himself and Great Dog. Spring was coming and he wanted to be on the baseball team. He also wanted to teach Great Dog to jump into the air and flip over before he caught a log, as he had seen his friend's dog do when his friend threw her a stick.

He would kill two birds with one stone. He began throwing the logs higher and higher. Great Dog jumped easily into the air, catching them, but he did not turn over. The problem is, thought Steven, that I'm not throwing them high enough. If I could throw them as high as the roof of the house, Great Dog would be able to flip over in the air. He went to the north wall of the house, which had no windows, and set about trying to throw the logs higher and higher. If I could just throw the log *over* the house, thought Steven. Then I'd be throwing it high enough for Great Dog *and* I'd know I was throwing well enough to make the baseball team. Great Dog looked at him encouragingly, as if he knew what he was thinking.

Steven looked at Great Dog and Great Dog looked at Steven. Steven picked up the log and prepared to throw it with all his strength. Great Dog prepared to leap up into the air, turn over and catch it. When Steven threw the log, it seemed to soar, as if it were lighter than air. It flew over the roof of the house! And there was Great Dog, also over the roof of the house, turning over in the air, catching the log in his teeth! Oh, what a wonderful day, thought Steven.

Inside, Foudini, who was watching, thought: time to run for the basement.

Outside, Great Dog lost his balance, and with the log in his mouth fell straight down, through the roof, through the two studies, right into the kitchen and the living room. Inside, Mr. and Mrs. Hood and June fled in three directions, like bugs surprised when their rock was turned over.

Great Dog shook himself, shedding bits of slate shingling, wooden siding, lathing, plaster and plaster dust, and looked around. He was standing with one front paw in the living room and one front paw in the kitchen. His back feet appeared to be outside. Mr. and Mrs. Hood were running toward him waving their arms, shouting, and pointing upward. Great Dog looked up and saw the sky. The ceiling was gone. He had fallen through it. The north wall of the house was also gone, as was the wall between the kitchen and living room. He had fallen through *everything*.

"What are we going to do now?" asked Mr. Hood. "We'll freeze to death! I told you it was too good to be true."

"When you're right, you're right," said Mrs. Hood.

"You could call Uncle George and ask him to help you rebuild it," said June.

"Build back half a house?" shouted Mr. Hood. "Half a house! I should call a doctor and get my head examined for keeping that dog!"

Great Dog lay down and put a paw over his eyes.

"Fred!" said Mrs. Hood. "I'm sure it was an accident."

"An accident!" said Mr. Hood. "Half the roof is off the house!"

"A large accident, it's true," said Mrs. Hood.

"I bet Steven had something to do with this," said June.

"Stop trying to get your brother into trouble," said Mrs. Hood.

"Well, why *was* Great Dog trying to jump over the house?" asked June.

"That's a good question," said Mr. Hood, putting on his parka.

"Don't talk to the boy while you're still so mad," said Mrs. Hood.

"I'm going to be mad for the next fifteen years," said Mr. Hood. He started to walk to the door when Steven came in.

"Um," said Steven. "He did catch the log."

"He caught the log, he caught the chimney, and he caught the roof!" thundered Mr. Hood. "Whose idea was this?"

"Mine," said Steven.

"Look at this!" said Mr. Hood. "HALF OF OUR HOUSE IS MISSING! The top half! Where are we supposed to sleep until it gets fixed? Do you have any idea of how much this is going to cost?"

"You could ask Uncle George to help you," said Steven. "We could sleep in the barn."

"Life," said Mr. Hood, "was more peaceful in the city."

"Not much," said Mrs. Hood.

"And when am I supposed to write if I'm building a house?" asked Mr. Hood.

"Only half a house, Dad," said June.

"At night, when you're not building," said Mrs. Hood.

"Sleeping in the barn isn't bad," said Steven. "It's warm in the barn."

The four Hoods looked at Great Dog. He was too large to fit through the front door. "Now what?" asked Mr. Hood.

June pointed to the roof, or what had been the roof. "Jump," she said, and Great Dog jumped over the wall and stood outside the house waiting for them.

"And where is that idiot cat?" asked Mr. Hood. Foudini, who had come up from the basement, mewed in the wreckage of the kitchen wall. Great Dog went over to him and the cat jumped up on his back. "I suppose that dog won't mind helping us carry food and supplies out into the barn?" asked Mr. Hood. Great Dog wagged his tail happily as if to say he'd be more than happy to help.

Mr. Hood went back into the roofless kitchen and called his brother, who refused to believe that a dog had jumped over the house. He said no dog was large enough to fall through a roof and he accused Mr. Hood of being drunk. Still, he said he would come up to help him. Business was slow in the winter and he didn't have anything better to do. "Fine, fine," said Mr. Hood, filling a plastic trash bag with some clothes. When he hung up, he dragged the bag over to the barn.

"Think of it this way," said Mrs. Hood. "You'll learn a new skill. If your books ever stop selling, you can build houses."

"Go to sleep," said her husband.

"It isn't so bad in the barn, is it?" asked Mrs. Hood.

Just then, June put Great Dog's dish of dried food and fried liver in front of him. Foudini had been watching all of this carefully, listening intently to every word that was said. He knew that Mr. Hood was upset. After all, who wouldn't be upset if someone fell through the roof of his house, letting in the rain and the snow and the wind? He wanted to cheer up Mr. Hood, and so he decided not to give his latest mouse to Great Dog, who, after all, had not behaved so very well that day. Instead of jumping over roofs, flipping in the air and catching silly logs, the dog should have taken down the bird's nest for him. So

31

Foudini brought his mouse over to Mr. Hood, who was falling asleep on the barn floor, and dropped it in front of him. "Oh, my God!" screamed Mr. Hood, jumping up and hopping down the barn floor in his sleeping bag. "Get that thing away from me!"

"He's afraid of a little mouse!" said June.

"Don't laugh at your father," said Mrs. Hood.

"That cat hates me!" said Mr. Hood. "I hate animals!"

Foudini heard this and went off into a corner of the barn where he sulked. Great Dog followed him and licked him, once again making his fur stand up in spikes. Don't worry, thought Foudini. From now on, *you're* getting all my mice. That man doesn't know what's good for him.

In the morning the house didn't look any better. Half of it seemed to have been destroyed by fire, and the roof had fallen in, but there were no signs of smoke. People from the town came by to look and said it was a good thing their horses didn't fly. People began stopping at the house to help clean up, to shut off the electricity leading to the ruined rooms, and to hammer in a board here and there. By the time Uncle George arrived, the house was in better repair than anyone would have believed possible. Uncle George and Mr. Hood got to work, and in a week the kitchen was just as it was, the roof over it fastened on tightly. By that time, Uncle George and Mr. Hood had acquired excellent reputations as builders, and Uncle George decided to move to the country. He had no idea, he said, that it was so beautiful or that it was so exciting. Great Dog, who was lying outside in the snow, sleeping, wagged his tail slightly.

The next day, the children were throwing snowballs at one another when their father rushed out, shouting and waving his arms. Under the impression that something terrible had happened, Uncle George rushed after him.

"Not near the house, not near the house!" Mr. Hood was shouting dementedly. "The dog! The dog!" When Uncle George caught up with Mr. Hood, Mr. Hood said that he was afraid the dog would try to catch a ball and crash through the living room wall. The children and the dog were sent to the edge of the meadow to play. All the dog could do there, said Mr. Hood, was deforest the place.

"But don't you ever wonder about that dog?" asked Uncle George.

"Of course I wonder about him," said Mr. Hood. "He's so gigantic I think he's descended from the dinosaurs."

"No," said Uncle George. "That's not what I mean. He's so big, maybe he has big powers."

"Powers?" said Mr. Hood. "What kind of powers?"

"Who knows?" said Uncle George. "But anyone can see he's not your usual dog. I bet he has them."

"Please!" said Mr. Hood. "He falls through roofs. His best friend is a cat. He carries school buses around. I don't want to hear about special powers!"

Uncle George shrugged. Foudini regarded Mr. Hood seriously, squinted, then delicately lifted one white paw to his mouth and began washing it.

"Look at that cat!" said Mr. Hood. "A spiked cat. A cat with a punk hairdo! Now you want me to think about a dog with powers?"

"Forget about it," said Uncle George.

Chapter 5

The Seam in the Sky

The house was once more whole, the roof was tight, and people again began marveling at how remarkably easy it was for a family to live with an animal the size of Great Dog. Mr. Hood regarded any such comments with suspicion because, in his experience, time around Great Dog was striped: there was the peaceful time, during which Great Dog slept in the barn and played with Foudini, ran across the meadow and fetched the logs Steven threw him, or stopped fights between the two children simply by walking between them, at which point they both fell gently to either side of the dog, and by the time they picked themselves up, they had forgotten what it was they were fighting about. The peaceful times were invariably followed by times of chaos, which Mr. Hood privately thought of as the black stripes of time. During these periods, school buses were found on the wrong sides of rivers, dogs, not asteroids, fell through roofs, he took up carpentry instead of writing books, and his brother began to wonder if the dog had magic powers.

There were times, Mr. Hood hated to admit, when he wondered the same thing. When he began repairing the roofless kitchen, for example, he noticed Great Dog standing outside, watching him through the pane of glass with an expression that could only be called satisfaction. That dog, thought Mr. Hood, looks like this was what he intended in the first place. He *likes* seeing me doing carpentry. Mr. Hood had to call the lumberyard to order more lumber, and as he dialed the number, he thought he must be imagining things. Probably all the dog was doing was laughing at him. The cat regarded him from a shelf that had, miraculously, stayed on the wall during what Mr. Hood called the dog-bombing. Foudini's look was severe, as if he meant to say that only a crazy person would talk into a tube fastened to a wall. Mr. Hood thought back to the city apartment that had once forbidden its occupants pets and wondered why he had ever moved. Just then the cat jumped down from the shelf, onto his shoulder, and butted his head into Mr. Hood's. Well, thought Mr. Hood, perhaps it was worth it after all: even if he had to live with animals who apparently could read his mind.

Right now, Mr. Hood was sitting in his favorite armchair, thinking about how peaceful it was, and how soon the peace was to end. Mrs. Hood's mother, who lived in Florida, had broken her ankle and his wife and June were going down to help her. This in itself was nothing to worry about. Mr. Hood, Steven, and Uncle George were perfectly capable of taking care of themselves, and Mrs. Hood's mother was getting better every day. He was worried about Great Dog's attitude toward family members taking vacations. At the first sight of a suitcase, Great Dog began to sit in front of the front door, blocking it. When he saw people near the side door, he ran to it and sat in front of it, blocking it. Chaining him to a tree was, of course, useless, since he would simply pull the tree out of the ground, drag it after him with roots dangling loose in the air, and plant himself *and* the tree in front of a door.

If the Hoods succeeded in outwitting Great Dog, and

getting themselves and their suitcases in a car, the dog would begin chasing them down the highway, and of course they would have to turn around and go back to the house because no one wanted to explain to a policeman how they happened to be going down the highway chased by a dog the size of a dinosaur. Once, they had managed to leave for a weekend. They had packed all their belongings into Hefty trash bags and carried them out to the car as if they were going to the dump, and as they hoped, Great Dog suspected nothing. However, Great Dog knew what they had done by the time they came back. Thereafter, whenever he saw the four Hoods taking garbage bags to the car, he sniffed them carefully. When he determined that the bags did indeed contain garbage, he lay down outside the barn and patiently waited for the four Hoods' return. How were they going to outwit Great Dog this time? Mr. Hood thought it was ridiculous to plot and scheme in order to fool a dog so that one could leave one's own house, but there it was.

This time, because only two members of the family were leaving, he was reasonably confident of succeeding. Empty suitcases were taken to Uncle George's, and each time the four Hoods went to the dump, they took some of June's and Mrs. Hood's clothing and stopped at their uncle's on the way home.

On the day the four Hoods left for the airport, Great Dog regarded them suspiciously, tilting his huge head this way and that, as if listening for something that would give him the answer to the question he was asking himself. When Mr. Hood and Steven returned and began cooking dinner, Great Dog was reassured and lay down outside the kitchen window, waiting for his dish of dried food and fried liver. He was still outside the window at midnight, waiting for Mrs. Hood and June. By morning, he realized they were gone. He went into the barn and would not come out. His dishes of liver and dry food went in and came out uneaten. Foudini danced around him, swatted at his nose, and even tried washing his ear, but the dog would not get up.

"There's only one thing to do," Steven said finally. "Call Grandma and let Great Dog talk to June."

"Don't be ridiculous," said his father.

"I think it will work," said Uncle George. "If there's one thing worse than a dog the size of a dinosaur, it's a dog the size of a dinosaur with his bones poking through his fur."

"You dial," Mr. Hood told Steven. The call was placed and Mrs. Hood answered.

"You mean you want me to talk to Great Dog?" she asked.

"You first, and then June," said Steven. He went outside and his father handed the receiver through the window. Then Steven called Great Dog, told him to lie down, and put the telephone near his ear. "Now talk," Steven told his mother. As he watched, Great Dog began reviving. First his ears stopped drooping and began to lift into the air until they were once again straight and pointed. Then his tail began slowly wagging. Finally, his tail was wagging so fast Steven had to jump out of the way. He took the phone from Great Dog's ear and listened.

"Oh, what a good dog, what a wonderful dog, what an adorable little puppy!" he heard his sister saying.

"That's enough," said Steven. "Great Dog feels better."

"I bet you're bored there," June said smugly. "*Here* it's hot and we go swimming in the pool every day."

"I'm not bored," said Steven, although he was.

"I bet the dog wouldn't stop eating if *you* left home," said June.

"I'm hanging up," said Steven.

"Don't hang up," said his father. "*I* want to talk to your mother."

"Now," said Ungle George, after Mr. Hood had hung up, "you can go on vacations without worrying. All you have to do is call the dog every day."

"Don't speak to me," said Mr. Hood. "Other people's children have horses." He looked over at Great Dog, who was playing happily with Foudini. The cat leaped onto his paw and off again.

"The Brontosaurus and the Mouse," said Uncle George.

Days passed and still June and Mrs. Hood did not return. Many of the children had gone to camp, or to visit relatives, or on trips with their family, and Steven was bored. He began to miss his sister, something he would not have believed possible. He was tired of throwing logs for Great Dog. He was tired of watching Foudini swing from his front paws from high barn beams in his tireless pursuit of the baby barn swallows.

At night, the distant mountains were blue and mysterious and occasionally at sunset a jet would fly through the clouds, its trail the orange color of the setting sun. I would be safe in the mountains, thought Steven, if I went with Great Dog. People say there are still black bears and even wild cats, but nothing is stupid enough to come close to Great Dog.

Steven told his father he was planning on camping overnight in the mountains and taking Great Dog with him. They would go deep into the deep mountains where there were no houses, because it was summer, and the country was full of city people, none of whom had ever seen or heard of Great Dog, and someone might mistake him for some kind of monster and take a shot at him. Great Dog listened to Steven tell this to Mr. Hood and seemed to be smiling.

It looks to me, thought Mr. Hood, as if that dog has plans of his own. "Are you taking the cat?" he asked his son.

"No," said Steven. "Great Dog is taking the cat."

"Naturally," said his father.

When his son, who was fifteen, set off for the deep woods and the high mountains, Mr. Hood did not worry about Steven at all. Instead, he breathed a sigh of sympathy for all the wild creatures who might encounter the boy, his dog, and the dog's cat.

Steven himself expected adventures in the forest, but an adventure would not *be* an adventure if it was something one could anticipate. Steven was surprised when he awakened and found a huge black bear staring down at him, but not at all surprised to see Great Dog open his mouth, pick the bear up in his teeth, and carry him, paws flailing, to the nearest stream where he proceeded to drop the bear into the water. He came upon three dogs chasing a deer, dogs that had been abandoned by summer people and then run wild, and just as one dog was about to latch onto the deer's rear leg, Great Dog said "WOOF!" The trees shook as if thunder had just shaken the sky, and the dogs took immediate flight. All this was delightful, but none of it very surprising, and occasionally Steven found himself looking at Great Dog with something like reproach. What possible adventures could he have accompanied by such a dog? Great Dog, who seemed to know what he was thinking, regarded him sadly, but kept running ahead through the trees, and then came running back as if he were certain that the boy, in the three seconds he had been gone, had managed to lose himself in the woods.

"I'm coming, I'm coming," said Steven grumpily, wondering what on earth Great Dog could be after now. The dog *was* after something. They climbed until they were above the tree line and then Steven sat down, told Great Dog to sit down, and took the huge sack of food from Great Dog's collar and ate his lunch: three peanut butter sandwiches, one thermos of lemonade, and four doughnuts. Foudini, who had been asleep in the sack of food, woke up, squinted, and looked around grumpily. Great Dog was happy with two peanut butter sandwiches and a drink of water from the creek, and Foudini was happy with his package of dried food, but as soon as they finished eating, he was eager to go on.

"Well, what now?" Steven asked impatiently. "There's nothing up here but sky."

Great Dog tilted his head toward the horizon and they kept on walking. They walked into the blue distance until the horizon suddenly stopped receding and seemed to stand still as they approached it. If I didn't know better, thought Steven, I'd say that wasn't a blue sky at all but a blue wall. He looked at Great Dog who was happily wagging his tail, waiting for Steven to follow him. When Steven came up to Great Dog and tried to walk past him, he found he could go no further. He had come to the place where the horizon ended, and where the horizon ended, the blue sky became a solid wall.

"I must be dreaming," Steven said aloud. Great Dog snorted. The dog pressed his head up against the blue wall of the horizon and began sniffing. Finally, he found what he was looking for: a seam in what appeared to be blue paper covering the wall. Great Dog looked at Steven to be certain the boy was watching him, and then carefully used his front teeth to pull at the blue seam of paper sky. Slowly, he began to peel the paper away from the wall.

Steven watched him, amazed. It was as if Great Dog were peeling back the sky itself. He looked around him: perhaps this was only a gigantic billboard someone had left up on top of the mountain? But it was no billboard.

Clouds floated by on the blue paper Great Dog was beginning to peel from the wall in larger and larger pieces. One piece was still hanging from the wall. This, thought Steven, is strange. But it was also familiar. And then he remembered the day he and June were peeling old wallpaper from the attic room and found the lathing behind it, the crumbling plaster, and behind it, Great Dog, who was then only a puppy the size of a shoebox.

"Is this how you got into our house?" Steven asked Great Dog. "I mean, are there places where you can go through from Here to There?"

Great Dog happily wagged his tail and peeled more blue paper. The blue pieces he dropped on the ground were the color of the sky, and in them, clouds floated lazily.

"The thing is," said Steven, "I know where *Here* is, but I don't know where *There* is." Great Dog licked Steven's face and wagged his tail. "When you're finished, are we going through?" Steven asked. Great Dog wagged his tail even faster. Foudini, who was asleep in the food bag hanging from Great Dog's collar, suddenly meowed loudly. "Are we taking the cat?" asked Steven. Great Dog's tail wagged so fast the branches in the trees below them began waving back and forth as if in a high wind.

Finally, Great Dog was finished. He nodded at the opening he had made in the blue sky and started walking toward it, waiting for Steven to follow him. Steven, however, was suddenly afraid. Who knew what was on the other side of the wall? "WOOF!" said Great Dog in his loudest voice, and Steven scampered through after him. He looked back for an instant to see if the pieces of blue sky with clouds floating on them still lay on the ground, but then he had to run to keep up with Great Dog.

The place he found himself in was strange. Everything was bathed in an orange-gold light, the color of the set-

The city came floating toward them.

ting sun, yet there was no sun visible anywhere. He seemed to be in an endless field, and he wondered what life was like on the other side of the sky. It seemed an empty place. There were no buildings, no people. And then he felt a warm wind rising and in front of his eyes, a *city* came floating toward them. "Woof!" said Great Dog happily. The city hovered above the field as lightly as dandelion seeds on the other side of the sky hover in the air, and then it settled in front of them.

At first, Steven thought it was a city very much like the one he had lived in before he moved to the country. It was filled with towering, shimmering buildings, and wide streets. But as he and Great Dog and Foudini got closer, he realized that everything in the city was infinitely larger than anything he had seen on the other side of the sky. Many dogs were walking up and down the streets, and most of them were two or three times larger than Great Dog, who looked like a puppy next to them. Steven looked around for people his own size but he didn't see any. He looked up at Great Dog, and then at one of the larger dogs, and he felt as if he had become smaller than the period at the end of one of the sentences he wrote in his notebook.

"Is this where you came from?" Steven asked.

"Woof," said Great Dog. "Yes."

"Yes?" Steven repeated. "Can you *talk?*"

"Only on this side," said Great Dog.

"Then tell me what we're doing here," Steven said.

"Going to see my mother," said Great Dog, as if it were the most natural thing in the world. "Climb up on my back or people will stare at you. No one here is used to human beings. Only one or two have ever come through this way, and they were pets."

"The people here were pets?" Steven asked.

"They were pets of the great dogs," said Great Dog. "If you don't want to climb up on my back, I could put

44

you on a leash and walk you along and then no one would bother you."

"I'd rather climb up," Steven said huffily.

They turned into a wide street where Great Dog said his mother lived.

"Um," said Steven, "I don't know if you've noticed this, Great Dog, but the city is *floating*."

"Oh, that's nothing," said Great Dog. "The city always floats unless it's coming down to pick someone up."

"I don't like this *at all*," said Steven.

"I don't either," said Foudini. "If you think you're small, I'm ridiculous."

"He can talk too?" Steven asked, astounded.

"On this side of the sky all animals can talk," said Great Dog.

"We can on the other side too," said Foudini. "You just don't know what we're talking about."

"Do people—I mean dogs—keep cats for pets here?" asked Steven.

"Certainly not," said Great Dog. "People here—I mean *dogs*—have *manners*."

Chapter 6

When Worlds Collide

Great Dog's mother lived in a house very much like the brownstone the four Hoods had lived in before moving to the country. "It's a very nice house," Steven said, surprised. "Not exactly what I expected."

"You thought we'd live in big dog houses," said Great Dog with a sigh. "People always do."

"Woof! Woof! Woof!" said Great Dog when he was at the top of the steps leading up to the front door. Then he scratched at the door three times.

"Murgatroyd!" said his mother when she came to the door. Her tail was wagging frantically, and she stood up on her hind legs and took Great Dog's face between her huge paws. "Just in time for your monthly visit!"

"Monthly visit?" said Steven. "But we've had Great Dog at our house almost nine months!"

"Isn't he cute?" Great Dog's mother said. "People are always cute, especially when they're small." She wagged her tail and looked at Steven in a friendly way.

The living room was filled with odd furniture, huge white circles that looked like half-filled balloons. "Go ahead," said Great Dog. "Sit down. They're very comfortable."

"Is that a *cat*?" asked Great Dog's mother, who had

"Murgatroyd!" said his mother.

just noticed Foudini. Foudini had unhooked himself and begun walking up and down Great Dog's back.

"Don't you like cats?" asked Steven.

"Cats are very nice," said Great Dog's mother, "but they're very rare here. Even more rare than people. Tell me your story," she said to Foudini.

"Well," said Foudini, puffing himself up importantly, licking a paw before beginning, in order to create the proper suspense.

"What story?" asked Steven. "Why should he have a story?"

"All animals have a story," said Great Dog's mother. "If they didn't have a story, they wouldn't end up on the other side."

"Does Great Dog have a story?" asked Steven.

"She asked about *my* story," said Foudini.

"Please tell your story," said Great Dog. "You never told it to me on the other side."

"Well," Foudini began looking around to be sure everyone was listening. "My mother knew there was going to be trouble in our city, and she went to the blind grandmother, who told her that all firstborn cats would soon be killed. So she decided to send me to the other side. The trouble was, when she sent me over, she didn't do enough research. It wasn't her fault. She was in a hurry. She put me through the first crack she could find."

"Crack?" asked Steven.

"In the *wall*," Foudini said impatiently.

"Like the one you and I went through to get here," Great Dog told Steven.

"Let me tell the story," said Foudini.

"Of course you are telling it," said Great Dog. "Please continue."

"Well," said Foudini again. "She put me through a

48

crack, as I said," and he looked around to be sure everyone was not only listening but watching him as he spoke.

"Yes," prompted Great Dog. "And then?"

"And on the other side it was the middle of winter. It was freezing cold. And there I was on the other side, with no one to tell me what to do, a very small kitten, only six months old." He paused to wipe a tear from his eye with his paw. "An orphan of the storm," he said.

"Terrible," said Great Dog's mother.

"But there might have been *worse* cracks," said Foudini. "After all, this crack was near a building in the town, and the door to the basement was open, so I went in. I remembered a story my mother told me about how it was always warmer inside buildings than outside."

"And right she was," said Great Dog's mother.

"So I made my way down and found myself in the boiler room," said Foudini, "but there was nothing there to eat. So I got into a box—at least I thought it was a box—and the next thing I knew, I was swimming for my life! I was going round and round!"

"A washing machine," said Great Dog.

"Of course I didn't know that at the time," said Foudini. "At the time, I thought I'd fallen into the ocean. And there was froth on the water and it burned my eyes and stopped up my ears. Oh, it was terrible."

"Soap," said Great Dog.

"I know," Steven told him.

"What happened next?" asked Great Dog's mother.

"The woman heard me shrieking in the middle of her wet clothes," said Foudini, "and she pulled me out. Of course, I scratched her, but the next thing I knew, I was in a cardboard box with holes in it. Then I woke up in this terrible place. I was in a big box with bars on it and there was a man in a white coat who kept sticking me with sharp needles and taking my temperature."

"A vet," said Steven.

"It's all very well for you to be so calm about it now," said Foudini, "but when it happened, I was just a kitten and I didn't know what any of it meant."

"And then?" said Great Dog.

"And then I got better, and they put white powder on me and all the bugs that bit me fell off and died, and then I escaped."

"Escaped?" said Steven.

"There was a truck," Foudini explained, "and one day the vet left the cage door open, and I hopped aboard the truck. I didn't see how it could be worse. And then the truck stopped at a house to deliver wood and I jumped out and decided to find the boiler room of that house. Of course, it didn't have one, so I went to the barn. And that was how I met your son," Foudini said to Great Dog's mother. "I had an unhappy childhood, wouldn't you say?" asked the cat.

"Cartons dropping on you, boiler rooms, needles, people taking your temperature, I should say so," agreed Great Dog's mother.

"But things have not been too bad at the four Hoods'," said Foudini. "Not *too* bad."

"How could they be better?" demanded Steven.

"Oh," said Foudini, calmly licking a paw, "there's always room for improvement. Another cat to play with would be nice. No cats come near the four Hood's house because they're afraid of *him*," said Foudini, looking over at Great Dog.

"It's true that on the other side my son does look large," said Great Dog's mother. "Here, of course, he is only a runt."

"Tell us Great Dog's story," asked Foudini. "There's a human being on the other side who calls your son a brontosaurus. Why did you send him over?"

"Well, as you know," said Great Dog's mother, "all

animals have their destiny. And when I learned that if Murgatroyd—pardon me, Great Dog—stayed here, he would be killed in a fight with his best friend, there was nothing I could do but put him through. Our house is very old, so old I knew it was built over a crack everyone else had forgotten. So I went into the summer kitchen and began digging through the wall, and then through the lathing, and finally I was almost finished, and I expected to see the blue sky on the other side, but instead, what did I see? I saw the lathing of a tiny wall on the other side, and I heard children's voices, and I thought, children always love puppies: I will take my chances. I will put him through here. So I put Great Dog inside the wall and then plastered up the wall on my side. Of course, once I put him through, I didn't know what happened to him, and I knew he couldn't come back for at least a month."

"Nine," said Steven. "Nine months."

Great Dog's mother smiled indulgently. "Has he been a good dog?" she asked Steven.

"Very good," said Steven. "Probably he shouldn't have carried the school bus across the river, but it wasn't his fault he crashed through the roof of our house."

"I will have to hear more about this later," said Great Dog's mother. "Now it's time to eat." She disappeared into the kitchen and emerged with a bowl in her teeth. It was a very small bowl, and she set it down in front of Foudini, who slid down Great Dog's side and began eating. A second bowl was for Great Dog, and a third, for Steven.

"What is it?" asked Steven, looking into his bowl.

"Fried liver and oats," said Great Dog. "Very good." He was already licking his bowl clean.

"Maybe later," said Steven. "I'm not hungry right now. I'm sure I will be in a little while." Great Dog looked at him, puzzled. Steven motioned to Great Dog, asking him to lower his head. "Do you have any dog biscuits?" Steven asked. "I think I'd prefer one of those."

"If you want a dog biscuit," said Great Dog, "you'll have to wait until we get back to the other side. We don't have dog biscuits here. I didn't know you liked them."

"A peculiar child," said Foudini.

Oh, boy, thought Steven.

Just then, everything started to shake. The floor heaved beneath Steven's feet, the walls of the room seemed to move out and then back in, and in the kitchen, he could hear things toppling from the walls.

"An earthquake?" asked Steven.

"Not exactly," said Great Dog's mother. "I'm afraid our city just hit another floating city."

"Is that bad?" asked Steven.

"Of course it's bad," said Foudini. Was the boy an idiot? "If cities bang into one another, can it be a good thing?"

Just then, another enormous *thump* shook the room and Steven found himself lying under Great Dog's paw looking up at Foudini, who was flying through the air over Great Dog's back on his way to the wall. Fortunately, Great Dog's mother caught the cat in her mouth and gently put him back on the floor. "I think," said his mother, "that this city is bumping into another city, bouncing away, and then bumping into it again."

"Doesn't anyone steer these cities?" asked Steven. "They can't just float around like soap bubbles."

"They do float around like soap bubbles," said Great Dog. "Whenever you and June blew soap bubbles in the meadow, it reminded me of home."

"But sometimes the bubbles would hit one another and both of them would burst," said Steven.

"Exactly," said Great Dog gloomily.

"This is how all our wars start," said Great Dog's

mother. "One city blames the other city for all this bumping and crashing, when really, it's no one's fault. The cities just *drift*. They've always drifted and sometimes they drift into one another."

"But if it's no one's fault," Steven began.

"The trouble is," said Great Dog's mother, "everyone wants to believe it's *someone's* fault. That's how dogs are."

THUMP! THUMP! THUMP! Foudini hurtled over Great Dog's ears and Steven reached up and caught him.

"Much obliged," said the cat, looking about with a displeased air. "Really," said Foudini, "life on this side is not as perfect as I remembered it."

"What can be done?" asked Steven.

"The usual thing," said Great Dog's mother. "One of the cities has to make a hole in its wall and get out of the way by sinking to the ground."

"How do they decide which city will do the sinking?" asked Steven.

"That's the trouble," said Great Dog's mother. "They often can't decide and then both cities bang together until their walls break and everyone falls out of the sky."

"We can't let *that* happen," said Steven.

"You're so smart, *you* think of something to do about it," said Foudini, his sharp little tail raised straight in the air.

"Quiet," said Great Dog's mother. She was listening, head tilted, ears up, to distant wails. As the first wails faded, the wailing sounds were repeated, this time louder and closer by. The third time she heard the wails, Great Dog's mother looked at them and said, "I'm afraid we're in serious trouble. The two cities seem stuck together. If one of the cities doesn't sink, we're going to be upside down and right side up and upside down again. Am I turning green? I *feel* green."

"I have an idea," said Steven. "How close are we to the edge of the city?"

"Two or three miles," said Great Dog. "Not far. Why are you staring at the cat that way?"

Foudini was walking back and forth, his little thin tail sharp in the air.

"Well," said Steven, "if you prick a balloon with a needle, it collapses."

"What does that have to do with me?" Foudini asked nervously.

"Doesn't his tail look awfully *sharp*?" Steven asked.

"It is a very nice tail," Foudini agreed.

"Not nice," said Steven. "It's *sharp*. Like a needle."

"Don't mention needles to me," said Foudini. "I had enough of needles when I was a mere kitten. An orphan of the storm. I can't tell you—"

"Not now you can't," said Steven. "We're going to the edge of the city and you're going to poke a hole in the city wall with your tail."

"I'm going *to poke a hole in the city wall with my tail*?" Foudini shrieked. "I'm not poking holes in anything! I don't want a whole city of dogs after me! I'm not crazy!"

"And after you poke the hole, you'll hide and we'll come back here and go back out through the crack behind Great Dog's kitchen wall."

"No," said Foudini.

"It will only take a little while. No one will be watching a cat's tail. It's sure to work."

"Forget it," said Foudini.

"Um, Foudeen," said Great Dog.

"Don't try to get on my good side using that nickname," said the cat.

"Let's try it," said Great Dog.

"Why should I listen to you?" shrieked the hysterical

cat. "You fall through roofs and swim away with school buses. You're just a runt!"

Great Dog turned on his side and faced the wall.

"Fine!" said Steven. "Now you've hurt his feelings!"

Thump! Thump! Thump! The cat flew overhead. "Catch me!" he shouted to Great Dog.

"Catch yourself," said Great Dog.

"I'll go!" shouted Foudini.

Great Dog caught him.

"What's everyone wailing about now?" asked Foudini, as he and Steven and Great Dog started off to find the city wall.

"The walls of buildings are starting to crack," said Great Dog. "So if you don't help, a building might fall on you."

"I *said* I'd help, didn't I?" said the cat grumpily. "Didn't I say I'd help? Do you have to go on about it? Do you have to talk about buildings falling on me? I'm a nervous cat. A person from a boiler room."

"Oh, shut up," said Steven.

"And I don't want a whole world of dogs to see what I'm doing and decide to tear me limb from limb," said the cat.

"He has a point," said Steven.

"You have to hide me," Foudini pleaded. "Don't you have a witch somewhere who can make me invisible?"

"No witches," said Great Dog. "Sorry."

"If you put him in your mouth," Steven began, but the cat interrupted him saying he was certainly not getting in that liver-smelling mouth, he was certainly not sitting on that wet tongue in the middle of those big white tusks Great Dog called teeth.

"Have it your own way," said Steven. "Just walk up to

the wall under everyone's nose and stick your tail in the wall."

"Under everyone's nose?" asked the cat.

"And eyes," said Steven.

"I'll get in his mouth," said Foudini. "Just don't forget I'm in there and bite down."

Ahead of him, two streets seemed to run into one another crazily, one ending and another standing straight up, as if it were a path into the sky. "I think we're at the wall," said Steven.

"Great," said Foudini from inside Great Dog's mouth. "I'm so happy."

"Quiet," said Steven.

"When do you want to let the air out of the other city?" asked Foudini.

"Not the other city," said Great Dog. "*This* city."

"This city!" shrieked Foudini. "They'll kill us! You'll kill your own friends and relations!"

"No one will get killed. The city will get heavier, pull loose, and settle on the ground. Calm down."

"I AM CALM!" shouted the cat.

Several huge dogs were inspecting the city wall. "We're stuck together, all right," said one of the dogs. "I hope they decide to collapse themselves soon."

"Can I see?" asked Great Dog. His voice sounded odd since the cat was sitting on his tongue.

"Look at the little dog," said one of the big dogs. "Sure. Come on over."

Great Dog went over to the wall and began licking it.

"Is that dog simpleminded?" one of the bigger dogs asked.

"It would seem so," said another.

"Now," Steven whispered to Foudini, "what you're supposed to do is back out of Great Dog's mouth. Don't fall off his tongue. Stick your tail straight out behind you

56

and keep going until Great Dog tells you to run back inside."

"I'm not doing it," said Foudini.

"If you don't do it," said Steven, "I'll tell Great Dog to drop you down right here. In front of all these really big dogs."

"Go ahead," said Foudini. "Drop me down. I dare you."

"Drop him," said Steven.

Great Dog opened his mouth and tilted his head down.

"All right, all right," the cat hissed. He backed down Great Dog's tongue until he was almost at the edge. "I'm going to fall off, I know I will."

"Just two more steps," said Great Dog.

"Just two more steps and I will never be heard of again," said Foudini.

"Be brave," said Steven.

Foudini took two more steps. His little tail pierced the wall and he flew back down Great Dog's tongue into the darkness of his mouth.

"What's that hissing?" asked one of the huge dogs.

"It's coming from over there, near that little dog," said another of the big dogs.

"You better get away from the wall," the big dog told Great Dog. "We've sprung a leak. Go home."

Great Dog jumped into the air, picked Steven up in his teeth, and bounded back to his mother's house. "We're going down!" he said. "We're safe!"

"Unless someone figures it out," said Foudini, who was wet and miserable and felt his fur becoming spiky all over. When he got out of Great Dog's mouth, he looked like a porcupine.

"Oh, well done," said Great Dog's mother. "Out the crack in the kitchen wall. It's time for you to go back."

"I think I'd like to stay for a while," said Steven. "It's

interesting here. We can go back later, through the same crack we came in."

"Well, if you're staying," said Great Dog's mother, "have some dinner," and she set a dish of fried liver and oats in front of him. Steven held his nose and began eating.

And so Steven saw the floating city settle. He and Great Dog and Foudini watched the other dogs repair the wall by blowing a thick white cloud through a pipe at the tear and then rubbing ice over the torn area. All this took several weeks, and then Great Dog announced it was time to go.

Steven had seen the humans some of the dogs kept as pets, and each time Steven saw a human pet, Great Dog would ask the boy if he recognized him.

"No," said Steven finally. "Why should I?"

"Well," said Great Dog, "sometimes when a person passes away on your side, he shows up on this side."

Steven said he thought people went to heaven.

Great Dog said there were all kinds of heavens.

Steven said he thought the other side was a pretty poor heaven if it was filled with perpetually colliding cities.

"You should see some of the other worlds on this side," said Great Dog. "A lot of people decide to come here. After."

"I wouldn't," Steven said.

"One never knows," said Great Dog.

"By the way," asked Steven, "will we be able to talk when we get back to the other side?"

"No," said Great Dog. "But you can ask me questions and I can scratch once for yes and twice for no."

"Why don't you just bark?" Steven asked.

"I have all kinds of things I bark about," said Great Dog. "It would get confusing."

"Don't expect me to start scratching in the dust," said Foudini. "I'm a busy person. I have my mice to catch. I have my own mother to visit. I have to take a *bath*. Look at this fur!"

"Cats are so vain," said Steven.

"But we are beautiful," said Foudini.

"Cats are so conceited," said Steven.

"If you were so beautiful, you'd be conceited too," replied the cat.

"I give up," the boy said.

Chapter 7

Tomato Juice

Steven, Great Dog, and Foudini were back on the other side, above the timberline, almost ten miles from home. Great Dog carefully picked up the pieces of the sky he had peeled from the blue wall and stuck them back in place, telling Steven to press them down neatly so none of the seams showed.

"I can understand what you're saying!" Steven exclaimed. "That's going to be trouble. We have enough of a problem explaining a dog your size, but a talking dog! Dad will go through the roof!"

"I'm not talking," said Great Dog. "I'm barking. You understand what I mean when I bark. That's because you spent so long on the other side."

"You mean other people only hear barking?" asked Steven.

"That's right," said Great Dog. "What about Foudini? Can you understand him?"

Steven picked Foudini up. "Say something," he said. He listened, but he didn't hear anything, not even a mew. Instead, a great deal of static seemed to be coming from the cat's throat. Foudini sounded like a defective radio.

"He's not saying anything," Steven said. The cat

hissed angrily at him and the noisy static became still louder.

"Well," said Great Dog, "maybe when he gets older, he'll do better." Insulted, the cat pushed against Steven's chest with his front paws and jumped down.

"Do you know what he's saying?" Steven asked Great Dog.

"I have a general idea," said Great Dog. "I can make out a word or two here and there. He's saying 'long walk,' 'tired,' and things like that. In short, he's complaining. Also something about a sore tail."

The static became even louder and angrier.

"I think," said Great Dog, "Foudini is trying to say that he speaks very well."

"On the other side, he said animals could talk to one another. If you could speak to him before," Steven asked, "why can't you now?"

"Well, to tell the truth," said Great Dog, "I never understood a word he said. He's not hard to figure out, you know. He's not the great mystery he thinks he is. I just guessed."

The cat looked at Great Dog with huge, insulted eyes and marched straight into the forest.

"We've got to go after him," said Steven. "He has absolutely no idea of the trouble he can get into there. He thinks raccoons will run away at the sight of him because whenever he's seen one, he's been with *you*. *You* frighten the raccoons off, but he thinks he does."

"It's living on islands that does it," said Great Dog. "All that dampness and fog get to the brain of a cat." He lay down and Steven climbed onto his back, hung onto his collar, and Great Dog galloped off into the forest. They didn't have long to look. A terrified shriek from the cat told them to turn left, and when they did, there was Foudini, not more than a few feet away, face to face with another black-and-white animal, this one with a white stripe running down its back and tail.

"A skunk!" said Steven. "Tell him to get away from it!"

"Get away from that skunk!" barked Great Dog. Steven had already pinched his nose shut because he'd noticed that skunks were the only animals who didn't seem to fear Great Dog.

"Foudini, get away from him!" Steven shouted. The cat looked at Steven, squinted nastily, and refused to move. The sound of static was distinctly audible.

"He's good and mad," said Great Dog. "He's insulted. You know how conceited he is. You can't do anything with him when his feelings are hurt."

"Let's get out of here," said Steven.

"And leave the cat?" asked Great Dog.

"What should we do?" asked Steven.

"Pray," said Great Dog.

"He's going to do something stupid," said Steven. "I know he is." And at that moment, Foudini stood up on his hind paws and shook his forepaws at the skunk, making it clear that he intended to attack.

"Oh, no," groaned Steven.

"Oh, NO!" moaned Great Dog, as the skunk turned around, lifted his tail, and sprayed the cat, Steven, and Great Dog.

"Now there are *two* reasons we can't go home!" cried Steven. "First, we've been gone for two weeks, and second, we smell to high heaven. Great Dog, what are you doing?"

The dog was scraping up wet moss from nearby rocks and stuffing what he could into his nose. "Noseplugs," said Great Dog. "We animals have very sensitive noses. I can't stand it."

"Scrape some moss for me," said Steven. Foudini was running around in circles, as if he thought he could leave the dreadful smell behind him. "Maybe you better scrape some moss for the cat," Steven said.

"Let him scrape his own moss," Great Dog answered in a nasal voice. Because his nose was stuffed with moss, he sounded as if he had a cold.

The cat, insulted again, began to stalk off into the woods, but Great Dog put out a paw, rested it gently on the cat's back, and pinned him to the ground. "Enough!" shouted Great Dog. "So you don't speak clearly on this side! Is that a reason to gas us all to death?" A burst of static answered his question. "I'm not *pretending* not to understand you," shouted Great Dog. "I *don't* understand you. Just a word here and there. When you grow up, you'll speak more clearly." The cat tried twisting around under Great Dog's paw so that he could swipe at him with his claws. Great Dog shook his head. "Cats can be impossible, you see."

"What are we going to tell my father?" asked Steven. "About the two weeks we've been gone? I've missed school. He'll never believe a word of it, the other side and all that stuff. He *won't*. He'll ground me until I'm old enough to get married."

"Don't worry about *that*," said Great Dog. "Time passes very quickly on the other side. We spent two weeks there, but here it's only two hours later. Everyone thinks we've been gone for a matter of hours."

There was another burst of static from Foudini, who was still lying on the ground under Great Dog's paw. "I think he's trying to tell me I'm an ignoramus and a runt," said Great Dog. "But I'm right about how long we've been gone."

"Now all we have to worry about is the smell," said Steven. "Maybe it's not as bad as we think."

But it was. As they began their long walk back through

63

the forest, they could hear animals fleeing in all directions.

"Don't worry," said Great Dog. "People don't have such a sharp sense of smell." But he didn't sound convinced.

When they got close to town, they began to hear windows banging shut. "Uh, oh," said Steven. "Humans may not have the best noses in the world, but they can certainly smell *us*."

They turned onto the main road and two children ran away from them, their hands over the mouths and noses.

"What's my father going to say?" Steven asked.

As it turned out, Mr. Hood was so overpowered by the smell that he began coughing and finally ran into the house, closed all the windows, went up to the second floor, and threw down Steven's sleeping bag. The sleeping bag was immediately followed by Steven's pup tent. "Stay out there until I find out what to do," Mr. Hood shouted. "Try washing in the creek." Then he slammed the window shut.

Foudini, Steven, and Great Dog went down to the river. Great Dog jumped in first, lay down in the water, then got up and shook himself. "How do I smell now?" he asked Steven. Steven took the moss from his nose, then hastily put it back. "I think you better try again," he said.

"And now?" asked Great Dog, shaking himself, sending a shower of crystal droplets through the air.

"I don't know," said Steven. "Maybe a *little* better." He put his hand to his nose, checking to see that the moss was still firmly in place.

"I'll try it now," said Steven. He jumped in the water. "It's cold!" When he was finished and had climbed out onto the bank, Great Dog removed the moss from one nostril, began to sniff, and pushed the moss back.

"Again?" asked Steven.

"Again," said Great Dog.

"Foudini, into the water," said Steven. Loud static, clearly a burst of protest, came from the bank and the cat retreated toward the house.

"Hmmm," said Great Dog grimly. He loped after the cat, picked him up in his teeth, clambered down the bank back into the creek, and began dunking the cat in the water. The cat's four paws flailed wildly, his claws extended, his little face indignant. The white lightning that streaked from his nose to his chin seemed even more jagged.

"He looks like a drowned rat," said Steven. This was too much for the cat. He covered his eyes with his paws and sobbed. "How does he smell?" Steven asked Great Dog.

"Like a skunk," said Great Dog.

"My father will think of something," said Steven.

Just then, Uncle George dropped by in his pickup truck. In the back, he had several old milk cans. Mr. Hood came out of the house.

"What's in those cans?" asked Mr. Hood.

"Tomato juice," said Uncle George. "It's the only thing that works. They all have to take a bath in it."

"There's only enough for Steven and the cat's tail," said Mr. Hood. "Where are we going to get enough tomato juice for Great Dog?"

Great Dog looked at them sadly with his huge brown eyes. Steven knew what he was thinking. He would have to go off into the woods and live alone forever. He couldn't even go back to the other side smelling as he now did.

"No tomato juice for me unless we get some for Great Dog," said Steven.

"Isn't that what I said?" asked Mr. Hood. "Didn't I say that we needed enough tomato juice for all of you? George, think of something!"

"Let's go in and make some phone calls," said Uncle George. Two hours later, they came out smiling. Uncle George got in his truck, and Mr. Hood backed *his* truck out of the shed. "If we build the wing on his house," said Uncle George, "Fontaine will give us his tomato crop."

"That's not a fair trade," Steven protested.

"Take out that nose plug and tell me that," said his father.

"In the meantime," said Uncle George, "stay *in* the water. If you can't stay in it, stay near it. Don't come too close to the house."

The three smelly creatures slunk off to the bottom of the meadow.

"This is terrible," said Steven.

"It's going to be worse," said Great Dog. Steven asked him *how* it could be worse. "It could be worse," said Great Dog, "because I'm allergic to tomatoes."

"You break out in hives?" asked Steven. "You itch?"

"I *sneeze*," said Great Dog.

Oh, fine, thought Steven. Tornadoes, gales, wind storms, trees falling over: these were the things that happened when Great Dog sneezed. "Are you sure?" Steven asked. At that moment, the two trucks full of tomatoes crossed the little bridge and headed up to the house.

"I feel a sneeze coming on!" said Great Dog. "Hold onto a tree! Hold the cat!" His nose was beginning to wrinkle. Suddenly, he sneezed, and Steven, who had one arm wrapped around Foudini and the other arm wrapped around a tree, was almost torn loose.

"I'm moving to Florida," said Mr. Hood before the first tomato juice bath was finished. "Better yet, I'm moving to Kansas. I'd miss all these tornadoes." Uncle George was standing at the far end of the meadow wearing Steven's football helmet. "Ready, George?" asked Mr. Hood. Uncle George nodded. Mr. Hood opened another milk cannister filled with tomato juice and Great

Dog sneezed again. The sneeze picked Foudini up and carried him like a football through the air. Uncle George kept his eye on the flying cat, saw where he would land, leaped up into the air, and caught him. "It's a good thing your uncle likes football," said Mr. Hood, "or that cat would be in California."

He took out his plastic noseplugs and sniffed. "Come on over here, Steven," he said. "We're not done yet. I never should have gotten married. I should have been a bachelor. Even if we get rid of the smell, how am I going to explain to your mother why your hair turned red?" He looked around him. The driveway was awash in tomato juice. "Whose fault was this anyway?" he asked. Steven, Foudini, and Great Dog looked innocently up at the sky. "I don't know why I ask," Mr. Hood said. "It's Great Dog's fault. It's always his fault."

Great Dog, who had a generous heart, said nothing.

"Is that your *mother* coming across the bridge?" asked Mr. Hood in horror. "*You* explain this to her," he told Steven. But Mrs. Hood already knew everything. She had stopped at the general store for a quart of milk, and the first thing she heard about was her son, Great Dog, and the skunk. The store owner told her he thought Great Dog had met up with Great Skunk.

"Don't make such a fuss," she told her husband. "Everyone meets a skunk sooner or later."

"The only skunk I've ever met is that big one over there," said Mr. Hood, pointing at Great Dog. "How one creature with only four feet can cause so much trouble is beyond me."

From Foudini came the loud sound of static.

"I know what he said this time," Great Dog said. "He called your father a name."

"What name?" asked Steven.

"Hitler," said Great Dog.

"Maybe we should tell my father what really happened," Steven suggested.

Foudini heard this and ran into the barn where he hid in his dark corner. He would not come out until morning, and so he missed the last of the tomato juice baths. As a result, when Steven and Great Dog smelled once more like themselves, people still fled when the little cat approached. In the end, Great Dog picked up the cat in his teeth and dunked him ten or eleven times in a vat of tomato juice.

"Two or three times would have been enough," said Steven.

"He *deserved* it," said Great Dog.

"What about June?" asked Steven. "Should I tell her about the other side?"

"Don't tell her," said Great Dog. "Humans aren't supposed to know anything about it. Promise."

"I'll never tell," Steven promised.

Chapter 8

Foudini Takes Off

June suspected something important had happened while she was in Florida, but Steven refused to tell her what it was. "But what did you *do* the whole time?" she asked, and Steven would always tell her the same thing: nothing. He and Great Dog had gone on walks and gotten bitten by mosquitoes and all in all were pretty bored. Except, of course, for the skunk and the tomato juice.

"Then why is the cat mad at you?" June asked.

"Foudini's always mad about something," Steven said.

"I never saw anyone sulk the way that cat does," said Great Dog.

"Me neither," Steven agreed.

"And that's another thing," said June. "You're always talking to yourself."

"No I'm not," Steven said.

"You just did. You said, 'Me neither.' Who were you talking to?"

"To you," Steven said, turning red. "You just said you never saw a cat get so mad. Don't you remember what you said?"

"I didn't say anything of the sort!" June said indignantly.

"You did," Steven insisted. He reminded himself again that only he could understand what Great Dog was *really* saying when he appeared to be barking, and if he kept answering the dog, people would think he was crazy.

"I didn't!" said June. "You're hearing voices! You're as nutty as a fruitcake!"

"Go to your rooms!" said Mrs. Hood, sticking her head out the living room window.

"You *are*," June whispered, as she passed Steven on her way to her room.

"*You're* the one who's crazy!" shouted Steven.

"I heard that!" said Mrs. Hood. "Steven, stay in that room until supper time."

"It's not fair!" Steven complained.

"I heard that too," said Mrs. Hood.

Great Dog waited until the house had quieted down and then thumped his nose against Steven's window. Steven opened the window and Great Dog stuck his nose in. Steven petted him, and Great Dog growled with contentment. "It's too bad, sometimes, that you're so large," Steven said. "If you were smaller you could come in and stay with me all afternoon."

From the hall landing, they heard the loud sound of static. Foudini was walking into June's room, his thin tail up in the air. *I* am small enough to go wherever I want, his tail seemed to say.

"What a nice cat! What a good cat!" said June. "What a wonderful little person!" From her room, came a loud staticky purr. "What a purr!" said June. "It was a normal purr when I left. Now you sound like a broken television. What happened to you?"

Across the hall, Steven and Great Dog sighed. "He'll get over it," Steven said. Great Dog shook his head slightly, as if to say he didn't think he would. "That cat is mad at us," said Great Dog. "Cats don't like water. They don't like baths in tomato juice. They don't like flying through the air like a football. They don't like being the only one not able to talk. He's up to something."

"Great Dog, stop that barking!" called Mrs. Hood.

"What *can* he be up to?" asked Steven. "He can't talk. He can't give us away. He can't take June back to the place where the sky comes loose. He can't walk that far and June would never go into those woods alone. Neither would he. Not after meeting that skunk."

"He'll think of something," said Great Dog in a low growl.

"Why is that dog growling?" called Mrs. Hood. "Go see if anyone's coming." No one was coming.

In June's room, Foudini was sneezing. "Oh, you poor thing!" June said. "You've caught cold!" Foudini sneezed again, even more loudly. "Are you sick?" June asked. Foudini sneezed, and sneezed again, then crawled into June's lap, rolled over on his back and dangled his paws in the air. Foudini was trying to say that he would find a way to get even with Great Dog and Steven yet, but June didn't know that. She thought the cat's chest was congested and that he had pneumonia. "Oh, you have to go to the vet," she said, and Foudini sneezed enthusiastically. "Mother!" called June. "Foudini's sick!"

"Call the vet," said her mother.

"The vet!" said Steven. "That's what he's up to. He said he came through from the other side in a crack near the vet's."

"Don't let him go," growled Great Dog.

"What's that dog growling about now?" called Mrs. Hood.

"There's nothing wrong with Foudini," Steven told her. "He's just pretending."

"A cat pretending to be sick?" asked Mrs. Hood. "Why? So he won't have to go to school?"

"Very funny, Ma," said Steven. "There's nothing wrong with him. His nose is cold."

"All he cares about is that dog," June complained. "He doesn't care if *my* cat gets sick and dies!"

"Be quiet, both of you!" called Mrs. Hood. "June, call the vet."

The vet said he would be out of the office the rest of the afternoon. He was visiting larger animals, horses and cows, nothing as large as Great Dog, of course, but he'd be in the office in the morning, and if it wasn't an emergency, they could bring the cat in then. When June reported what the vet said, Foudini was not pleased. He wanted to go to the vet's at night because there would be fewer people about. If they waited until Saturday morning, there would be more people. It would be bright daylight and everyone would be able to see what he was up to. In the dark, a black cat could get about easily. At night, he was practically invisible. He began sneezing wildly and tried to say, "I'll get even with the two of you now," as loud as he could, so that his staticky purr would further alarm June.

"It's an emergency, Ma!" called June. "I think he's dying."

Mrs. Hood, who was painting a windowsill, sighed, put her brush into the can of turpentine, untied the kerchief over her curly red hair, and went into the shed to get the cat's traveling box.

"All right," she said, coming into June's room. "Let's go."

The cat sneezed and roared with static. "Good Heavens," exclaimed Mrs. Hood. "I hope he lives long enough to get to the vet's."

"I want to come, too," said Steven. "I'm very worried about that cat."

"You said he was only *pretending*," June said.

"I must have been out of my mind," said Steven.

"No," Mrs. Hood said. "You stay home. With Great Dog."

"But Ma!" said Steven.

"Don't 'But Ma' me," retorted Mrs. Hood. "You stay here with your tomato-souped friend." She and June got in the car, Foudini's carrying case in between them. From his bedroom window, Steven watched the car pull away and cross the little cement bridge. He and Great Dog sighed together.

"Don't worry," said Great Dog. "He's not smart enough to get into trouble."

"I don't know about that," Steven said. "Foudini is conceited, but he's not stupid."

The vet listened to Foudini sneezing, and then put his stethoscope to the little cat's staticky chest. "I don't know what to make of it," the vet said. "Maybe he swallowed something."

"Like what?" asked June. "A radio?"

"Don't be fresh," said Mrs. Hood.

The vet said he thought he better keep the cat overnight, whereupon June burst into tears and said she wanted to stay also, especially since the vet would be leaving to visit the sick horses he'd mentioned earlier. She'd sleep on the couch in the waiting room. Mrs. Hood said she'd do no such thing, but her daughter could stay at the vet's for a couple of hours while she did some shopping. "Fine," said the vet, carrying a squirming Foudini off to a large mesh cage. He said he'd be back by seven and Mrs. Hood could pick June up and then he'd lock up.

"Now, whatever you do," said Mrs. Hood, as she zipped up her parka, "DON'T OPEN THAT CAT'S CAGE."

"She wouldn't do that," said the vet. "She's a smart girl."

But as soon as Mrs. Hood and the vet had gone, Foudini began crying in a piteous voice. The cage he was in was exactly like the cage he had been in as a small kitten. He was once more locked up in the place from which he had been so proud of escaping. June pulled a chair up to his cage and began petting him through the bars. Foudini squeezed up against them, trying to rub against the child's hand. This went on for almost half an hour and finally June could stand it no longer.

"I don't see what harm it would do if I opened the cage and stuck my arm in to pet you," she said. "I really don't see what harm that would do." So she unlatched the cage door, put in her hand, and began stroking the cat. Foudini, who was certainly no fool, hung onto her arm as if were the last log afloat on a stormy sea, and began wailing his heart out. He looked at June with hurt, frightened eyes. "I don't see what harm it would do if I took you out and held you," said June. "I really don't see how that could do any harm." And she opened the door and reached in for the cat.

But before she could pick him up, Foudini jumped out of the cage, stood in the middle of the floor, his thin tail erect, and wailed at June. Then he walked to the rear of the room. June, who didn't see any harm in the cat walking about, followed him. She found Foudini scratching at what looked like a small trapdoor in the wall. "I wonder what that's for," she said. "It looks like a door for animals." She unfastened the latch and looked through the crack between the door and wall. "Oh," she said. "It *is* a doorway for animals. They can go right from here into the yard." She opened the door a bit more. "I think *I* could fit through this," June said. Just then Foudini streaked through the small doorway in front of her. She saw him leap across the yard and she *thought* she saw the white stripe of his nose pause on the far side. Without thinking, June went out the door and followed him.

Foudini saw June coming, waited until she was almost within reach of his tail, and then skipped through the hole in the yard fence. "Wait! Wait!" June called. She was too large, she saw, to fit through the hole in the yard fence, but she saw that she could climb over it if she stood on top of an overturned wheelbarrow. Once she climbed over, Foudini would run ahead of her, then stop, waiting until she almost caught up with him, and then run on. If I didn't know better, thought June, I'd think he was trying to take me somewhere.

Finally the cat stopped near an old building and began clawing at something. June, who was out of breath, caught up with him and sat down on the ground. "What are you doing now, you monster?" she asked the cat. "You're not acting like a sick cat, you know." The cat looked at her disgustedly and continued scratching. June began to pay attention to what Foudini was doing.

The cat seemed to be clawing at the dark air immediately next to the building. The cat's crazy, she thought. But, she thought, it *sounds* as if he's scratching at something. Just then, Foudini leaped into the air as he did when he first caught sight of a mouse, and began clawing rapidly with his front paws. June watched, fascinated. Finally, Foudini tilted his head, seemed to catch the darkness in his teeth, and began pulling it toward him. June had never seen an animal so intent on anything before and she crept closer to the cat and put out her hand to touch the darkness the cat seemed to be attacking. But she did not feel air. She felt something solid.

"Air solid as a wall!" she said aloud. The cat rumbled happily with static. June saw an odd, misty, gray light behind the solid, black wall. "There's something there!" June said. She went over to the cat and put her hand on the piece of dark air the cat seemed to be pulling loose from a very strange wall. "I'll pull some away, too!" said June.

When she and Foudini finished, they had made a hole in the darkness big enough to crawl through. On the other side, they could see what looked like a meadow covered in thick gray mists. From the other side of the darkness, the dampness blew against their skin. Foudini bounded through, mewing for June to follow him. Mother won't like this, she thought, hesitating. But at last, she stepped through after the cat.

June and Foudini found themselves in the middle of a huge field in which the mists were swirling like living things, taking the form of one animal after another. Protruding through the mists, June could see enormous brown cat tails. A cloud shaped like an enormous gray cat swirled across the field toward them, as if it intended to pounce upon them where they stood.

"Where are we?" asked June.

"In cat country," said Foudini.

"You can talk!" June exclaimed.

"Let's not go through that again," said Foudini. "Yes. Yes. All animals can talk on this side."

"But what are we doing here?" June asked the cat.

"Going to see *my* mother," said Foudini. "Why should that Great Oaf go see his mother when I have to stay on the other side so sick with homesickness I can barely endure it? A poor little thing like me. I didn't want to visit *his* mother. I wanted to visit *my* mother."

June had no idea what the cat was talking about, but assumed she would find out eventually. In the meantime, Foudini was following the mist-shaped cat. "Where are we going *now?*" she asked him.

"To the shore, of course," said Foudini. "We're almost there. You can hear the waves if you perk up your ears."

June listened and heard the sound of waves crashing. "I don't like this," she said. "I get seasick in the bathtub."

"We're not going *swimming*," the cat said contemptuously. "We're waiting for my city."

"What is it, a boat?" asked June.

"A boat!" sniffed Foudini. "It's one of the floating cities."

"How do you know it will float up to us here?" June asked him.

"My *mother* knows I'm here," said Foudini. "Of course she'll send the city to come and get me."

"It's so damp my clothes are getting wet," said June.

"Don't complain," said the cat.

"What *is* that?" June asked, staring into the mist. *Something* was approaching the shore. "It looks like an island. A very *muddy* island. All I can see are cat tails and grass. It doesn't look like a city to me."

The cat sighed. Humans! They didn't know anything. "The city," said Foudini, "is *underground*." June wanted to know why on earth anyone would build a city underground. "Grant me patience!" said the cat. "Cats are always at war with one another. When my tribe moved to this island, everyone decided to live underground. The spirit cats stay on the surface, but if you're underground, you're safe. At least, most of the time you're safe."

"Spirit cats?" asked June.

"Cats that look like *spirits*," said Foudini. "Don't you know *anything*?"

"Well, pardon me," said June.

"Never mind that," said Foudini. "Get ready to jump. The island moves away fast after it touches the mainland. I don't want to fall in. Jump!" Foudini jumped and seemed to disappear into the ground. June jumped in after him. The cat leaped onto her shoulder and pulled some kind of door shut over them. "You saw it?" Foudini asked her. "The spirit cat?"

"I didn't see anything," said June.

"You didn't see its slanty eyes? You didn't notice it looked Egyptian?"

"I don't know what you're talking about," June said, annoyed. "There are no such things as Egyptian cats."

"There are," Foudini insisted. "We learn about them in school. The Egyptians worshiped cats and taught them magic spells and wrapped them up and made them into mummies. The Egyptian cats live forever and they can float like clouds and they can kill you just by looking at you."

"Ridiculous," said June. "The Egyptians thought cats were gods. That's why they worshiped them. They didn't teach them magic tricks."

"You have your history book, I have mine," said the cat. "Besides, I *saw* the spirit cat. It wanted to kill me."

"Oh, nonsense," said June. "Why should anyone want to kill you?"

"Not *just* me," said Foudini, "although I am a very important cat, being a firstborn. Egyptian cats don't like firstborn cats, especially ones as handsome as I am. They want to kill *everyone* who lives on the island."

"But why?" asked June.

"Because they always have."

"But why did they always want to?" asked June.

"*Because,*" said Foudini.

They were creeping down a narrow, low tunnel when the cat suddenly stopped and tapped against a little wooden door. Three taps, then two taps. Three taps and then two taps again. A door opened and June found herself looking into the face of the largest gray cat she'd ever seen. "He's a guard cat," Foudini said huffily. "*He's* big. *I'm* not small. He's completely overgrown. A monster, so to speak."

The guard cat nodded as they passed him.

"How does he know you belong here?" asked June.

"Because, anyone stupid enough to come here belongs here. Anyone who isn't a spirit cat and knows about the tunnels belongs here. *And* anyone who sees me knows at once that I belong anywhere. It's my personality. First-born children often have such a gift. After all, *you* took me in when I turned up. I could have gone *anywhere.* Anyone would have taken me, as I well know. Of course, I would have preferred to remain here, but my mother heard that the spirit cats were after firstborn kittens, and she knew they'd want me more than any other kitten, so she sent me away."

"Are firstborn cats also smart cats?" asked June.

"Of course they are," Foudini answered.

"Then how do you know the spirit cats have finished with the firstborn kittens? I mean, did your mother send you a message? Is there some kind of mail that goes from one side to the other?"

"You mean," asked Foudini, staring at her, "that the attack might not be over? They might still be after me?"

"Well, we don't know, do we?"

"You mean right now all those spirit cats might be looking for *me?*" asked Foudini.

"Not just you," June reminded him.

"I want to go back to the barn," Foudini said.

"You should have thought of that before you decided to play sick," June told him. "Let's start back now."

"We can't, we can't," said the cat, flinging himself down on the ground, starting to cry. "The island won't float back to the mainland for two days. My life is over. I began as an orphan of the storm and I'll end as an orphan of the storm."

"You'll end as a fur rug if you don't get up this minute," said June. "*I'll* turn you into a fur rug." Foudini lifted his paws from his eyes, saw she was serious, and got up.

79

"We could look for my mother," he whimpered. "*If* she's still alive."

"Let's go," said June.

They were standing in something resembling a brightly lit closet.

"Don't you have any streets here?" asked June.

"*Of course* we have streets," said the cat. "You have to leave this chamber and then you can walk on them. Just because we live underground doesn't mean we don't have an outside and an inside."

"*Where* is OUTSIDE?" June shouted at him.

"This way," said the cat, walking in front of her. "Here's the door. It's painted white. It's hard to see if you're not a cat."

Foudini and June found themselves on a broad, brightly lit street. June thought it looked less like a street than a huge tunnel, but it was lined with trees, and in each tree were several huge tree houses. On the branches of the trees, June could see cat after cat, sound asleep. "Three o'clock," Foudini said smugly. "All cats sleep from three to four. Then it will be lunchtime. Delicious food! We'll be at my mother's soon." The cat's tail rose straight in the air.

They walked until June was tired, past what seemed to be miles and miles of trees, their branches lined with sleeping cats, and the tunnel wound this way and that, at times seeming to double back on itself, at other times going uphill or downhill. "We'll never find our way out again," said June, who was beginning to worry.

"I could find my way back with my eyes closed," sniffed the cat. "With my eyes closed *and* my nose stuffed up. With my eyes closed and my nose stopped and my ears clogged . . ."

"Enough!" said June. She was hungry. She thought about the peanut butter and jelly sandwiches she made at home, the pizza and the ice cream in her freezer, and began to feel sorry for herself.

"Here we are," said Foudini. They were in front of the most enormous tree she had ever seen. Its boughs were each thick enough to be tree trunks and its topmost branches were so high they seemed to be holding up all of creation. Foudini saw June admiring the tree. "I come from a very old family," he said proudly. "The older your family, the bigger your tree. Mother!" he shouted.

A large tiger cat poked her head out of the topmost tree house. "Mythylmroyd, is that you?" asked a sleepy voice.

"I'm home. Your troubles are over," called Foudini.

"Mythylmroyd?" asked June.

"Never mind that," said the cat.

"Bring your friend up," said the cat's mother. Foudini looked at June and remembered that although June could climb trees, she got dizzy easily, and even when they were harvesting apples, she stayed on the lowest branches.

"You live up there?" asked June. "All the way up there?"

"All the way up there," replied Foudini. "Follow me and don't look down."

"I can't do it," June said.

"Put your shoes in your mouth and climb up," Foudini told her.

"I can climb in sneakers," said June.

"Let's go," ordered the cat. "Follow me. It's very easy. Extend your claws."

"I don't *have* claws," June wailed, beginning to climb.

"We're almost there," said the cat. "Think of lunch. Delicious lunch. Wonderful lunch. My mother is the best cook in the world." June thought about lunch and climbed until she was in front of the green door of

Foudini's house. Once inside, she collapsed on the floor and felt her chest to see if her heart was still beating. It was like Foudini, she thought, to live on *top* of the underground.

"But you have to go back," Foudini's mother was saying. "The spirit cats haven't left yet. They'll know you're back, they always know, and they'll come after you."

"How will they know?" asked June.

"They always know," said Foudini's mother. "They have magic powers."

"But he's safe down here, isn't he?" asked June.

"When he was a newborn kitten, I told him he'd always be safe down here. But the spirit cats often get in. They can come down here."

Just then it grew dark outside the window. "A cloud," said June.

"A cloud?" said Foudini. "Underground?"

"A spirit cat," said his mother.

June looked out the window. An enormous cat, apparently made of fog and mist, moved slowly through the branches of their tree. "Into the cupboard!" Foudini's mother told her son. "Not you," she said to June. "They're not interested in humans. Not that there's anything wrong with humans, you understand, but they're not *cats*."

"Are you in?" she asked Foudini. "Did you pull your tail around you? Good." And she slammed the cupboard door. "Now he'll have to stay in there until it's almost time for the island to touch the floor," his mother said. "*You*," she called to Foudini. "You don't *deserve* any supper. There are worse things than baths in tomato soup. A dunking in tomato soup is not the end of the world. Which is worse, a dunking in tomato soup, or a spirit cat tearing you limb from limb? And when you know perfectly well that if they find you here, the rest of us will be in trouble!"

Foudini cried quietly in the closet.

"And bringing this poor, hungry girl with you, a poor thing without claws who can't climb trees! I hope," she said to June, "that you like fish." She set a huge dish of fish-head soup in front of June, and looked nervously out the window. The cloud was gone. "I'm sure it's better than what you're used to," she told the girl.

June had never seen or smelled anything that looked worse.

"It's so good I'd rather save it for later," she said. "Is there anything else?"

"More fish-head soup," said Foudini's mother. "It's so good, I always have pots and pots of it."

June sighed and began eating her soup. She found it tasted better if she held her nose while she ate. Foudini's mother observed her, and decided that human beings had very strange table manners. Just then, a misty paw, claws extended, reached into the window of the tree house. One of the claws caught in June's sweater.

"Help!" shrieked June. But at the sound of June's very human voice, the misty paw began shaking itself, freed its claw, and slowly withdrew from the window. "Will it come back?" asked June.

The misty paw crept in through another window and began groping through the room. "I'm the only one who lives here," June cried out. "I scared the cats away." The paw hesitated and then withdrew. "It's gone," June announced, and Foudini's mother came out of the cupboard where she'd been hiding with her son.

"But it will come back," said Mother cat. "You have to hide in the tunnels until the time is up. I'll pack you a bag of dried fish and fish heads. They're even better than the soup."

"I suppose we wait until dark," said June.

"No," said Mother cat. "It's never dark down here.

But at three in the morning and three in the afternoon, all cats sleep, even the spirit cats. First, you must get in the tunnel. Then you must wait until the island floats back to the mainland. If you're there before four o'clock, you'll be able to get back without the spirit cats finding you. You won't have any trouble finding the mainland. After all, you have my *son* for a guide."

At three o'clock that morning, they went back through the mazelike streets and were soon back in the tunnel. "I'm hungry," said Foudini. "I'm always hungry. I think I should be in charge of the food bag. You're so much bigger than I am. You might eat it all up."

"I won't," said June.

"You will," Foudini insisted.

"I won't. I don't like fish heads."

"Ha!" said Foudini. "*Everyone* likes fish heads!"

June looked at the bag of dried fish and fish heads. Two days in the tunnel with that smelly bag and that conceited cat! She didn't know if she could stand it. "How are we supposed to know when it's three A.M.?" she asked Foudini. "I was so worried about you I didn't put on my watch before we went to the vet's."

"We cats always know what time it is," Foudini said smugly.

"Fine. Wake me up when it's time to go." She leaned back against the wall. "The walls of the tunnel are soft," June said. "Like pillows." Then it occured to her that if the spirit cats could get into the underground city, they could also get into the tunnel. "Can those foggy cats get in here?" she asked, sitting up straight.

"Not this part of the tunnel," said Foudini. "They don't know about this part."

June asked him if he was sure. He said he was. She was tired and hungry and decided to take his word for it. He couldn't be wrong *all* the time. In a few minutes, she was sound asleep. When she awakened, the bag of dried fish and fish heads was almost empty, and Foudini, his stomach so swollen it resembled a round, Turkish pillow, was sound asleep on his back, his paws in the air. "Wake up!" said June. "What time is it?"

"Time?" said Foudini, licking his lips, thinking of fish heads. "Time!" he shouted. "It's almost four o'clock! We're late!"

He and June quickly ran down the tunnel, opened the trap door, and once more found themselves in the thick, damp mist. "Run!" said Foudini. "The island's already at the mainland! It's starting to move away!"

The mists around them seemed to thicken. He and June looked up and found themselves surrounded by spirit cats. They were huge and their eyes glittered like ice in the sun, and their mouths, showing their sharp teeth, were open.

"I don't believe in spirits," June said, as if the spirit cats might hear her, decide they were not really there at all, and conveniently vanish. But one of them swiped at her and she felt its claw against her skin. "What are we going to do now?" she asked Foudini. "I think they're going to eat us!"

He shook his head, pulled a dried fish head from the bag, and began chewing on it. "You're eating?" June asked him. "We're about to be eaten and you're *eating*?" The little cat looked at her, took out another fish head, and popped it into his mouth.

Furious, June plunged her hand into her pocket where she'd hidden a dried fish head in case Foudini ate all the food while she slept. She wanted to throw the fish head at him. But when she put her hand in her pocket, she didn't find the fish head. She found her cap pistol. She wondered if the sound of it would frighten the spirit cats. It always frightened her, even when she was firing it. At the sharp, loud sound the spirit cats jumped into

She began firing the pistol.

the air, ran away from them back toward the tunnel, away from the shore.

"Hurry up!" June shouted to Foudini.

She and the cat ran to the edge of the island, but the mainland was moving quickly away from them.

"Jump in the water!" June told the cat.

"I can't swim!" cried the cat. "I don't like water! You can't jump in either! Look! There's a shark!"

June looked behind her. The spirit cats had lost their fear and were returning. But when she looked in the water, she didn't see a shark. She saw two enormous pointed ears. "Great Dog!" she shouted. And out of the water bounded the huge dog, with Steven clinging to his collar.

Great Dog bent down and Steven slid over his head to the ground. Then Great Dog went after the largest of the spirit cats. "That won't do any good, you Great Oaf!" called Foudini. "They're made out of fog!"

"No, they're not," said Great Dog, who had his teeth into one spirit cat. "Watch this!" He began shaking the spirit cat back and forth until they heard a ripping sound. Out of the foggy, misty material fell a small, gray cat. The small, gray cat faced Great Dog for an instant, the fur on its back standing straight up, and then turned and fled. The other spirit cats went with him. Great Dog bounded after them and one by one he shook them from their costumes.

"They were ordinary cats," Foudini said, astonished.

"Naturally," said Great Dog. "If you had a nose like mine, you would have known that right away."

"But the mainland!" cried June. "How will we get back?"

"On my back, of course," said Great Dog. June and Steven climbed up and held onto his collar.

"Don't forget me!" said Foudini.

"I won't," said Great Dog, picking the cat up in his mouth. He dove into the water and began to swim.

"The land's getting closer," said June.

"Mmmm," said Great Dog. Every few minutes, he dunked Foudini into the water and shook the cat slightly.

"Stop! Oaf! Idiot! Loon!" cried the cat. "I'll tell my *mother!*" he cried desperately. Great Dog dunked him again. And then they reached land, and Great Dog climbed out of the water, carrying everyone with him.

"But how did you know where we were?" June asked. "How did you know *when* to come?"

"We didn't," said Steven. "We left as soon as we guessed what happened. You're going to catch it," he said to his sister. "Ma's furious at you. She thinks some-one kidnapped you *and* the cat."

"Don't mention that cat to me," said June.

Foudini began whimpering. He knew that his fur was wet and that he looked like a plucked chicken. "No one likes me," he wept. "Even my mother sent me away. I'll find the crack. I'll go back and let the spirit cats get me. Even if they're not real spirits, they can kill me all the same."

The three of them looked at Foudini. "I probably shouldn't say this," Steven said, "but we all love you."

"Hmmph," said Great Dog, vigorously shaking him-self so that water flew in all directions, soaking them all again.

"*All?*" asked Foudini, looking nervously at Great Dog.

"All," said June.

"Even *him?*" Foudini asked, pointing at Great Dog?

"Even me," said Great Dog. "Let's go home."

"This time can I ride on your back?" asked the cat.

"Be my guest," said the dog.

"When you swim, you create quite a wake," complained the cat. "I was soaked *all the time*. You didn't have to swim so fast. After all, I'm delicate. I'm only a cat. A mere orphan of the storm."

"Oh, shut up!" said Steven and June together.

"He's back to normal," sighed Great Dog.

"Is that a good thing?" asked June.

Chapter 9

What a Book Is For

Mrs. Hood was standing in front of the house, looking anxiously down the road, her arms folded across her chest, when Great Dog came trotting up, June and Steven on his back, Foudini clinging to June's neck.

"Where have you been?" she demanded of June. "Your father's out looking for you. The vet's looking for you. The state troopers are looking for you."

"The cat got loose and I went to look for him," June said, talking as fast as she could.

"You mean to tell me that cat picked the lock and walked out of his cage all by himself?" asked her mother.

"Not exactly," said June.

"Exactly how did he get out?" asked Mrs. Hood.

"Well, he was crying, and I felt sorry for him, so I thought, well, I'd just open the door a crack . . ."

"In other words, you let him out," said Mrs. Hood. "Didn't I tell you not to open that cage under any circumstances?"

"But these were *special* circumstances," June said.

"Grounded," said Mrs. Hood. "Grounded until you get married. Grounded until this time next year." She peered at all of them, sitting on top of Great Dog. "Are all of you *wet*?" she asked. "You look *wet*."

"Only damp, Ma," said Steven.

"And how did you get damp?" asked Mrs. Hood.

"We slid into the river chasing the cat," said Great Dog.

"Why is that dog always growling?" asked Mrs. Hood. "Sometimes I think he's trying to talk. *He'd* make a lot more sense than you kids do. Let me ask again. How did you get wet?"

"We slid into the river chasing the cat," said Steven.

"You can go change your clothes and go slide into the barn," said Mrs. Hood. "You can go slide into the barn every single day after school. No television, no radio, nothing but homework. If the two of you spend any more time traveling around the country with that barking dinosaur, you won't be able to read."

"Don't hurt the dog's feelings," said June.

"The dog can't understand English," said Mrs. Hood.

"She doesn't mean it. She's only angry," said Great Dog.

"Growl, growl, growl," growled Mrs. Hood. "Growl, growl, and growl again."

"Can we eat supper before we go into the barn?" asked June.

"No, you can't," said her mother. "You can eat supper in the barn. With Great Dog and with your *books*. And if there's any trouble, and I mean *any* trouble, falling walls, people getting wet inside the barn when it's not raining, you two will study in the chicken coop. No playing with Great Dog for a month."

"We'll behave!" said Steven and June together.

"Go wash your hair first," said Mrs. Hood, watching her children as they slid down the dog's nose. "The river must have been awfully muddy. June, that looks like *seaweed* in your hair."

"Don't be silly, Ma," said June. "There's no seaweed in the river."

*   *   *

For two days, Steven and June studied in the barn while Foudini chased mice in the dark corners or pounced on bits of bark that fell from the logs stacked for firewood against one wall. On the third day, Foudini sat in a dark corner watching the two children with their books. He saw how absorbed they were, and squinted with annoyance. His tail twitched. I'll just find out what's so interesting about those things, he thought. He pretended to stalk something to the side of the children, and then casually walked over and sat down on one page of June's book.

"Why do you keep looking at it?" he asked crossly. "It doesn't move. It doesn't change."

"You know," said Steven, "I think I'm starting to understand what he's saying."

"I've understood him since we went into that horrible, foggy place," said June.

"He's getting clearer," agreed Great Dog. "I think I understood every third word."

"Say that again, Foudini," said Steven.

"Why do you keep looking at that page?" asked the cat. "It doesn't move. I don't know why I have to repeat myself all the time," he complained, "when everyone immediately understands the Great Oaf."

"I understood him!" said Steven. "Every word!"

"You did?" asked Foudini, so pleased he flopped down on his side, completely covering the book, flexing his claws.

"You wanted to know why we're looking at something that doesn't move," said Steven.

"Well, why are you?" asked the cat.

"Because we can read," said Steven. "We read the words and in our minds we see pictures. Sometimes we read the words and see people and hear them talking. It's like magic."

"Cats can read," said Foudini, "but they don't have books like *that*. They have stone tablets and they draw little pictures on them and then they read the pictures. I don't see writing on those things you're looking at."

"It *is* writing," said June. "Maybe it's different than cat writing."

"Cats don't write," said Steven.

"They do," said Foudini. "The Egyptians taught us."

"Egyptians again," said June.

"I think there's something to it," said Great Dog. "My mother used to tell me stories about how the cats who lived on the floating island knew how to read."

"Can *you* read?" Steven asked Great Dog.

"The dogs don't even have books in their foolish bubbles," Foudini said.

"I never tried," said Great Dog. "I *think* I could learn to read."

"Well, you can't, no matter what you think," scoffed Foudini. "Only cats can read."

"You can't read our books," June pointed out.

"They aren't proper books," said the cat.

"I'll try," said Great Dog. "I *could* learn."

"Let's teach him!" June said.

"If you're going to teach him, you have to teach me," said Foudini. "You can't leave me out of everything just because I'm so small and you can forget I'm here. I'm more than a piece of dust, you know! *He* gets all the attention, carrying school buses and jumping through roofs and swimming around in the water like a shark. It's not fair!"

"We'll teach both of you," said Steven.

"We'll *try*," said June.

"Me first," Foudini insisted.

"Oh, brother," said Steven.

"The trouble is," said June, "we can't go back into the

house until bedtime. That's where the beginner's books are."

"But the old blackboard is out here," said Steven, "and if we got behind the woodpile, Ma wouldn't know what we were doing."

"It's never going to work," said June. "Some people don't have the patience for things like reading. Some *people* will quit after the second letter in the alphabet. Some *people* will decide to give up and chase mice and see to it that no one else can concentrate."

Foudini walked over to the woodpile, climbed to the top, and glared at her.

"Let's get started," Steven said. He had written out the first five letters and explained their sounds when Foudini, who was listening intently, craning forward trying to see the blackboard, lost his balance and slipped, starting an avalanche of logs.

"Why don't you just come over here?" asked Steven.

"Some *people* wait to be invited," said Foudini.

"You're invited," said June.

Foudini sat down next to Great Dog, but he found he had to tilt his head too far back to see the blackboard, so he got up and sat behind Great Dog.

"When you put the letters together," Steven explained, "you get a word. What is C-A-T?"

"Cat," Foudini said promptly. "This is interesting."

Steven looked at June. "It's an accident," she said. "He just assumes everything is about him. You know how he is."

"B-E-G," wrote Steven.

"Beg," said the cat. "This is easy." He waited eagerly for Steven to write something else on the board. "Why is everyone staring at me?" asked Foudini. "Write something else."

"Let Great Dog try the next one," Steven said. "D-O-G," he wrote.

"Um," mused Great Dog. "Let me think." Foudini's tail began twitching and he started his staticky humming. "I'll get it eventually, I'm sure I will," said Great Dog.

"Eventually!" said Foudini.

"Dig?" asked Great Dog.

"Dog, you idiot!" shouted Foudini. June said if he couldn't behave, he'd have to stay in another corner of the barn. He would have to cooperate.

"Cooperate?" asked the cat incredulously. "*Cats* don't cooperate."

"They do," said Steven. "If they don't cooperate, they don't learn to read." Foudini wanted to know just what he had to do to cooperate. June said he had to keep quiet while Great Dog tried sounding out the words. Foudini said that was a great deal to ask. Steven pointed to the far corner of the barn, and Foudini said that even though keeping quiet was a great deal to ask, he would try. *Under the circumstances.* Steven said he had to succeed, not merely try. Great Dog said he was tired of the discussion, and could they get on with it?

In the next few weeks, Foudini proved to be a rapid learner. By the end of the third week, he was reading third-grade textbooks, and by the end of the seventh week, he was reading June's and Steven's schoolbooks and asking for more interesting stories. Great Dog, on the other hand, was slowly stumbling through *Dick and Jane*. "See Spot run," he would read aloud. "Run, run, run." Then he would pause, look up, hang his head, and ask, "Is that right?"

"It's right," said June.

"It's right, Dodo," said Foudini.

"Get up on the woodpile," June told the cat. "One more insult like that and I won't look in the study for the books you want. You'll be stuck with these schoolbooks forever."

"But he's so *slow!*" complained the cat.

"One more word," June warned him again.

"Why don't you help teach him, then?" Steven asked. "You're here with him all day while we're in school and both of you are up after we've gone to sleep."

"You want *me*, a poor thing the size of a comma, to teach that *thing*, the size of a cloud?" asked the cat.

"You could try," said Steven.

"Well," considered Foudini, licking his paw, looking down at the floor.

"He wants us to beg him," said June.

"I wouldn't mind some help," said Great Dog. "I still mix up my b's and d's. They look the same to me. And he's so good at it."

"If you put it that way," said Foudini.

Mrs. Hood, who was coming back from the mailbox, looked in the barn window. "You know," she told Mr. Hood, when she went into the house, "I just looked in the barn and it looked as if the cat and dog were reading and the children weren't."

Mr. Hood asked her what she meant. She said that Great Dog had a book between his paws, and Foudini was picking up the pages with his claws and turning them.

"Oh, they play with everything," said Mr. Hood. "The cat sits on the table while we eat."

"But still," said Mrs. Hood.

"Still, nothing," said Mr. Hood. "That dog's so large, *nothing* seems normal when he's around. Your imagination is running wild."

"I suppose it is," sighed Mrs. Hood.

In the barn, Foudini, who had finished reading *Volume A to C* of *The Encyclopaedia Brittanica*, looked up and announced that since he could read so well he wanted to learn to write. After all, he had many stories to tell about his early life in the boiler room, about his adventures on This Side with people who read from books made out of paper, not to mention his recent visit to his homeland and his triumphant victory over the spirit cats.

"*Your* triumphant victory over the spirit cats?" asked June. "I thought *Great Dog* battled the spirit cats."

"Whatever," said Foudini, waving a paw. "I would like to write down my life story. I don't know anyone who's had a more interesting life."

June said reading was one thing and writing was another. How, she asked him, was he going to hold a pencil or pen in his *paw*? Foudini said he preferred to think of the object in question as his *hand*. June put a pencil against his paw and told him to try holding it. The pencil rolled from his paw and clattered against the wooden floor. Foudini went over to the pencil, looked at his front paws, and then picked the pencil up between both paws. He looked triumphantly up at June. But when he tried to write, the pencil began to slip backward through his paw, until it was once more on the ground.

"You see?" said June. "It's hopeless."

"What I need," said Foudini, "is a typewriter." He could, he said, extend his claws and use them the way humans used fingers. June said his claws weren't strong enough to press down typewriter keys. "They're strong enough for an *electric* typewriter," Foudini said.

"I'm not bringing Dad's typewriter out here," said Steven.

"When he's not home, I could go in there," Foudini suggested.

"Do *you* want to write?" Steven asked Great Dog.

"'Hop, hop, hop, said Peter Robot,'" Great Dog read aloud.

"Rabbit, not robot," said Foudini.

"I think I better work on my reading first," said Great Dog.

"*Can* I try the typewriter?" asked Foudini.

"Next time Mom and Dad go into town," said Steven. "Then we'll see."

Once Steven switched on the typewriter, Foudini had no trouble with it. The difficulty would be in persuading the cat to tear himself away from the machine. He sat up on his hind legs and busily typed with his front paws.

"What's he writing?" asked Great Dog, watching enviously through the window.

"I don't know. He says we can't look until he's finished," Steven said.

"You better tell him he's finished now," said Great Dog, "because I can hear your parents' pickup coming over the bridge."

When Foudini refused to give up the typewriter, June pulled out the plug.

"Now you've done it!" cried Foudini. "Just as I've gotten to the very best part! Right in the middle of an artistic fit! Just as my muses settled on each of my whiskers! IT IS IMPOSSIBLE TO BE A CAT AND AN ARTIST IN THIS HOUSE!"

June hastily gathered together the typed sheets, replaced the typewriter cover, and all of them fled to the barn. They heard the pickup truck pull up in front of the house. "From now on," said June, "if you want to use the typewriter, you have to stop when we tell you to! I don't care about muses! Is it a deal or isn't it a deal?"

"It's a deal," said Foudini.

"Can we read what you wrote now?" asked Steven.

"I will read it aloud myself," announced the cat.

"Hmmph," said Great Dog.

"Go *on*," said June.

"I began life very small," read Foudini. "From the beginning, I was an orphan of the storm. No sooner did I look about me and begin to recognize the tree houses of my country than danger struck and my heartbroken mother had to thrust me through a crack to The Other Side. This was, of course, understandable. I was so precious I had to be saved at all costs."

"Oh, brother!" groaned Steven.

"Oh, brother!" moaned June.

"Here we go again!" sighed Great Dog.

"I *knew* you'd like it," said Foudini. "Wait until you get to the part where I save the world."

"I can't stand it," said Steven and June together.

"*You're* the ones who taught him to read," Great Dog reminded them. The two children stared at him. Great Dog had never before sounded annoyed.

"You'll be able to write soon enough," said Steven.

"No, I won't," said Great Dog sadly. "One tap of my nail on that typewriter and the machine would turn to dust. Where would I find a typewriter large enough to write on?"

The children regarded him sorrowfully. They said they would think of something, but they couldn't imagine *what* they could think of.

"In my country," said Great Dog, "no one writes things down. We learn the stories and pass them down from generation to generation. I'll do the same thing. I don't mind. After all, I *can* read."

"So to speak," said Foudini.

"I looked in the barn window again," said Mrs. Hood.

"And what did you think you saw this time?" asked Mr. Hood.

"I thought I saw Great Dog trying to write in the dust with a huge log tied between his front paws."

"Next you'll go into the study and think you see the cat at the typewriter."

"When that happens," said Mrs. Hood, "I think I'll go see a doctor."

"Still, I don't know what's gotten into the children. All they do is read and write."

"Don't complain," said Mrs. Hood. "Baseball season's starting. By the way, were you up typing last night?"

"No," said Mr. Hood. "Why?"

"Oh, I thought I heard someone typing."

"A ghost," said Mr. Hood.

"A ghost who types very fast," Mrs. Hood said.

Chapter 10

The First Public Reading

Mr. Hood was becoming nervous. It was very, very quiet in the house. In the afternoons, the children always did their homework in the barn with Great Dog and Foudini. When Mr. Hood brought Great Dog his morning meal, the dog often didn't come out to get it. Instead, he lay quietly on the barn floor, his head on one of the children's books. But when he felt Great Dog's nose, it was cold. Apparently he was healthy. The cat, too, was behaving oddly. Whenever Mr. Hood went into his study, the cat was there. And the cat had developed an annoying habit of throwing books down from the shelves and playing with the pages. He didn't harm the books, but Mr. Hood worried that one day the cat would begin chewing on the pages as he had when he was a kitten. Perhaps, thought Mr. Hood, there was something wrong with the cat. During the day when he was usually to be found chasing mice in the barn, or hiding in the day lilies looking for toads, he was inside, playing with books in his study. But at three-thirty, when the school bus crossed the cement bridge to drop off June and Steven, Foudini and Great Dog were always standing outside waiting for them, the dog's tail waving

The cat, too, was behaving oddly.

madly, the cat, as usual, using the dog's tail for a jump rope.

There was, thought Mr. Hood, something wrong with *all* of them. The children neglected their friends and came straight home from school instead of going to baseball and basketball practice and went into the barn with the dog and the cat. What was most peculiar, Mr. Hood thought, was how quiet it was. He tiptoed over to the barn, looked in the window, and saw Steven, June, and Great Dog looking at Foudini as if they were listening to him. Mr. Hood decided not to tell his wife he thought everyone was too quiet. Whenever he did that, disaster was sure to follow.

Inside the barn, Foudini waited impatiently while Steven read aloud what he had written during the afternoon.

"It's a very good story," Steven told the cat. "I especially like the part where the two children and the two animals take revenge on the spirit cats."

"That's not a story," said Foudini. "That's a *plan*."

"A plan?" asked June.

"Great Dog thinks we should do it, too, don't you?" Foudini asked Great Dog.

"Do what?" asked Great Dog, who was reading *The Three Musketeers*. In the last weeks, he had begun reading faster and faster, and now only rarely stopped to ask Foudini what a word meant. Soon he would catch up with the cat.

"You think we should follow my plan to keep the spirit cats from ever *ever* attacking the cats of my city again," Foudini said.

"I said we should *think* about it," Great Dog corrected.

"If you think as slowly as you read, we'll never do anything!" exclaimed the cat.

"Quiet!" said Steven. "I'm trying to write!"

"No one else has to write now that *I'm* writing," said Foudini. "Now that *I'm* writing there's nothing else left to say."

"Good grief, what a conceited creature," said June.

"I *have* to write something for English class," said Steven. "Otherwise I won't get promoted. This is what I've written so far." And Steven held up a half-page of much-crossed-out, ink-blotted writing. "I can't write stories," Steven complained.

"Use mine," said Foudini in a sudden burst of generosity. "I don't mind at all. Doesn't your teacher read the best one out loud to the class?"

"We each read our stories out loud. I can't take your story," said Steven. "It wouldn't be right."

"You could take mine and write your own later," offered Foudini, who was completely taken with the idea of his story being read aloud to a roomful of children.

"It's not a bad idea," said Steven.

"It's not a good one," said Great Dog.

"What's wrong with it?" asked June.

"Something always goes wrong with Foudini's ideas," said Great Dog.

"Jealous! Jealous! *Jealous!*" cried Foudini. "All because no one wants to read *your* stories."

"That's not fair," said June. "You know we don't have a typewriter big enough for Great Dog."

"It wouldn't make the slightest difference," said the cat. "Dogs can't tell stories."

"You want me to hand in a story about a cat who goes back to his own city and rescues it from spirit cats?" asked Steven. "The teacher will never believe I wrote it. It's too good."

"Naturally," said Foudini.

"And all wrong," said Great Dog. "The spirit cats would have torn you apart if we hadn't gotten there."

"Like the cavalry," said June. "In the nick of time."

"Cavalry? Cavalry?" said Foudini. "Give me the dictionary. I have to look that up."

"Don't do it," Great Dog told Steven.

Steven said he would try to write a story once again, but if he failed, he would hand in Foudini's. Of course, he would have to copy it over in his own handwriting. Everyone knew he couldn't type.

"Brainless pea," Foudini muttered to himself.

"Oh, shut up," said Great Dog and June.

"We should never have taught him to read in the first place," said June.

"Too late now," said Foudini smugly.

"It's no use," said Steven, throwing down his pen. "I'm going to use his story."

"I can see trouble coming right now," said Great Dog.

"Envious beast," said Foudini. "Great Oaf."

"Enough," said June.

Steven handed in his story, entitled "Foudini and the Ghost Cats." His teacher congratulated him for handing his assignment in on time. "I told you so," said Foudini. But the next day, his teacher had him stay after school. She said she didn't believe he had written the story himself.

"But I did," said Steven. "I wrote down every word myself."

"I think you might have copied it from a book," his teacher said. "Or read it in a book and *accidentally* wrote the same thing. Is that possible?"

"No," said Steven.

"Do you swear to me that you didn't copy this from a book?" asked his teacher. "No good ever comes from lying."

"I swear I didn't find this in a book," said Steven.

"Then tomorrow you'll read it aloud to the class."

"Tomorrow?" asked Foudini. "Tomorrow you'll be reading *my* story to the eager world?"

"To the fifteen students in my class," said Steven.

"I want to listen to you read it," said Foudini. "A *premier performance* of my best work!"

"You can't come to school," said Steven, "and that's that."

"In your bookbag or something?" asked Foudini.

"Nowhere near the school," said Steven. "Stay near the barn *all day* tomorrow."

"I think I'm still small enough to fit into the pocket of your parka," said Foudini. "Don't you hang your coats on the hooks in back of the classroom? I wouldn't need much while I'm in your pocket. Just a morsel or two of dry food."

"Forget it," said Steven. "It's almost the end of the term. I don't want any trouble."

"Or you could take a lunch box and drill a *little tiny* hole in the side," suggested the cat.

"Forget it!" said Steven and June together.

"Dinner!" called Mrs. Hood, and the two children went back into the house.

"Well," said Foudini to Great Dog, "are you going to let them get away with that?"

"With what?" asked Great Dog.

"With not letting us hear our story read out loud," said the cat.

"*Our* story?" asked Great Dog.

"Well, it is about what happened to *us*," said Foudini. "*You* were the one who came to our rescue."

"You forgot that part when you wrote the story," Great Dog reminded him.

"Poetic license," said the cat. "But *we* know the truth. *We* want to hear our story, don't we?"

"*We* want to stay home and go for a walk in the woods," said Great Dog. "*We* want to go swimming in the river."

A tear trickled down the cat's cheek.

"Don't try to make me feel sorry for you," said Great Dog.

"Why would I do that?" asked the cat. "No one ever feels sorry for me. No one cares about me at all. Everyone hates me because I read so well. Don't think I don't know why Steven won't take me to school. Don't think I don't know why you won't go. You're jealous! You thought I was a stupid little thing, and now you're jealous! WAAAH!" cried the cat, flinging himself down upon the floor.

"All right!" said Great Dog.

"All right, what?" asked Foudini.

"All right, we'll go," said Great Dog.

"You'll take me?" asked the cat.

"We'll both go," said Great Dog. "We'll listen at the window. And as soon as Steven's finished reading, we'll come straight back home. Agreed?"

"Oh, agreed," the cat purred happily.

"You're always so much more pleasant when you get your way," said Great Dog.

"Who isn't?" asked the cat.

With Foudini on his back, Great Dog went over the tops of the hills until he and the cat looked down at June and Steven's school. "Now," said Great Dog, "we'll listen *quietly* at the window. We won't shriek with joy when we hear our story being read."

"*My* story," said Foudini. Great Dog sighed. He trotted down the hill toward the school and took up his position outside Steven's classroom window. The teacher was writing on the board, and the children looked up and saw him, waved, and when the teacher turned around to look at the class, they looked straight ahead. One after another went up to the front of the room and began reading. "This is *boring*," said Foudini. "What terrible stories! Why doesn't the teacher stop them and get on to the good one?"

Great Dog shook his head slightly. Foudini dug his claws into Great Dog's fur. "All right, all right," he hissed. "I'll be quiet. Don't do that anymore."

Finally, it was Steven's turn to read. The story was more interesting than Great Dog had remembered. He leaned closer and closer in order to hear better. The students, who were listening intently to the story, didn't notice that the building was beginning to list, like a sinking ship. The pencils on their desk were rolling to the edge, and they automatically pushed them back, whereupon they began rolling off again, this time more quickly. Steven had now reached the point in the story where Foudini, wielding a sword that had magically appeared out of nowhere, was chasing the spirit cats away. Great Dog leaned closer. This time the students' desks began sliding into the north wall of the school room. The teacher, too, began sliding. She grabbed onto the chalk tray of the blackboard and looked around her.

"The school is falling over!" she shouted. "Everyone out of the building!" The students, oddly enough, were not frightened, but were laughing. "This is an emergency!" the teacher screamed. "What's the matter with all of you?" Steven finally looked up from his paper, and saw Great Dog peering through the window, and Foudini, perched happily on his nose, was listening raptly.

"Oh, no!" said Steven. "I told you to stay home!"

"Are you speaking to me?" the teacher asked indignantly.

"To the *dog*!" said Steven. "Great Dog! You're toppling the school!"

"The school is falling over!" she cried.

Startled, Great Dog jumped back, the school settled on the ground with an enormous thump, and students and desks went bumping through the air.

When the teacher collected herself, counted all the students, and assured herself that no one was hurt, she looked out the window again. The huge dog had retreated to the top of the hill overlooking the school. "I must be dreaming," said the teacher. "I've *heard* about a dog as big as a dinosaur, but naturally, I never believed it."

"Naturally," said the students.

"I still don't believe my eyes," the teacher said.

"Believe what?" the students asked.

"Believe there's a huge dog there on top of the hill."

"Where?" asked the students.

"There," answered the teacher, pointing.

But Great Dog was gone.

"Maybe," said Steven hopefully, "it *was* your imagination."

"Isn't that huge dog *your* dog?" asked the teacher.

"I do have a huge dog," Steven admitted.

"I want to talk to your parents," said the teacher. "*In the morning.*"

"He came to hear me read the story," Steven said. "He and my cat think they wrote it."

"Go down to the doctor's office," said the teacher.

"What for?" asked Steven.

"Just go," the teacher said.

"We have to do what?" asked Mrs. Hood.

"You have to come to school and promise Great Dog won't follow me to school again," said Steven.

"I don't understand why he followed you in the first place," said Mr. Hood.

"Because I forgot my lunch," Steven explained.

111

"You always forget your lunch," said his mother, "and the dog doesn't follow you to school."

"He won't do it again," said Steven. "I promise."

"Someone could have gotten *hurt*," said Mrs. Hood.

"In the city," observed Mr. Hood, "all we had to worry about were criminals."

"He wasn't trying to misbehave," said Steven.

"It's a good thing people around here like that animal," said Mr. Hood. "I don't know why they like him, but they do."

"Everyone always feels safe when there's a large dog around," said Mrs. Hood. "That must be why."

"How could anyone feel safe with a dog *this* large?" asked Mr. Hood.

"*I* do," said Mrs. Hood. "I don't worry about anything when he's here."

"First the school bus, now the school," said Mr. Hood. "What next?"

"Don't *worry* so much," said Mrs. Hood.

"What time do we have to be in school?" asked Mr. Hood.

"Eight o'clock," said Steven.

"Eight o'clock!" exclaimed Mr. Hood. "Is no day safe from that dog?"

"There's nothing to worry about *now*," said Mrs. Hood. "It's always quiet after they get into trouble."

"That's what you think," said Mr. Hood.

"We'll be good," June promised.

"Likely story," said her father.

Chapter 11

What to Do?

"But this is the *perfect* time to go to The Other Side," Foudini said. "No one expects us to do anything. You heard your mother. They think everything's going to be quiet for a while."

"And they're right," said June. "They just went to see the teacher this morning. We *have* to behave."

"But now is when we should go," insisted Foudini. "I feel it in my bones."

"Great Dog, what do you think?" asked June. She was sure he would say they should stay home and keep quiet.

"It's a crazy plan," said Great Dog. "But cats are crazy. It might work."

"See!" exclaimed Foudini. "Let's get busy."

"But where are we going to get two cement tablets?" asked June.

"We don't need cement tablets," said Foudini. "We only need two large pieces of granite and Great Dog can scratch the words on them. I'll trace the words in the dust and he can copy them."

"Letters?" asked Great Dog.

"Well, not exactly," said Foudini. "Hieroglyphs. That's what they call the picture-letters cats read."

"I'd rather try letters," said Great Dog.

"Explain it again," said June.

"We'll get two stone tablets, and we'll write a message on them," Foudini began. "We'll tell them they're forbidden to wear those spirit-cat suits and we'll tell them that they can't attack any of the floating cities anymore or they'll be destroyed. They'll believe it. We'll say we found two sacred Egyptian tablets. They still believe the Egyptians are gods."

"I don't know," said June. "Even though there were small cats inside those spirit suits, they were *very* strong. And *very* mean. I don't trust them."

"We can do it, can't we, Great Dog?" asked Foudini. "You write out the tablets and you frighten the spirit cats, and I'll do all the thinking. It's sure to work."

"Well," said Great Dog, "I would like to try writing."

"You can try writing without going back to the kingdom of the cats," June said. She shivered, remembering how damp and cold it was, especially on the ground, above the tunnels.

"The spirit cats *are* bad," agreed Great Dog. "Someone ought to teach them a lesson."

"Not us," said Steven. "You and Foudini follow us to school and *we* get the extra homework."

"I'm not going," said June.

The cat watched them and licked his front paw. "Then I'll go by myself," he said.

Steven, June, and Foudini waited while Great Dog peeled back a patch of gray sky behind the veterinarian's building. "I can't believe this," said Steven. "I can't believe we're going to deliberately look for the spirit cats."

"We can go through now," said Great Dog.

"Oh, terrific," said June as she moved closer to the opening. "I can feel the damp wind already. I can see the cat tails."

"Come *on*, June," urged Steven, and then they were all on The Other Side. Great Dog reached through, picked up the pieces of gray sky he had peeled away, and pressed them back in place. A little light shone through, but no one would notice.

"How long do we have to wait before the spirit cats' island gets here?" June asked.

"Ummm," said Foudini.

"How *long*?" asked Steven.

"Well, there's something I forgot to tell you," said Foudini. "The spirit cats' island doesn't move from place to place. We'll have to swim over to it."

"WHAT!" cried Steven and June together.

"*You* can't swim," Great Dog reminded the cat.

"I didn't mean *I* would swim," said Foudini, "not when you swim so well. I expected you to carry us there. You're so strong. *Such* a good swimmer. *Such* a brave dog."

"Enough," said Great Dog.

"You want him to carry us *and* the two tablets?" Steven asked. "We'll all sink."

"The Great Oaf will not sink," Foudini insisted.

"If I have to carry you through the sea to the island," said Great Dog, "have the good grace to stop calling me names."

"Sorry," mumbled Foudini.

"Say it louder," said June.

"I'm sorry!" shouted the cat.

And the next thing they knew, Great Dog was paddling through the churning gray sea toward an even grayer, more miserable-looking island. "Keep the tablets out of the water!" Foudini called to Great Dog. "I don't want them dissolving."

"Granite doesn't dissolve," said Great Dog. "I read all about granite in the *Encyclopaedia*."

"Considering how you read," Foudini said sarcastically. June reminded him that if it weren't for Great Dog, he would be sinking to the bottom of the ocean. The cat kept quiet.

"When we get there," Steven asked, "how are we going to find the spirit cats?"

"They have sentinels all over their shoreline," said Foudini. "They'll find us."

"Terrific," said June. "What if they don't feel like reading stone tablets? What if they decide to tear us apart and eat us?"

"Then Great Dog will bark at them," said the cat.

"Thanks a lot," said Great Dog. He didn't like the spirit cats. They made him nervous. In fact, if the truth were told, they frightened him.

Chapter 12

Suits of the Spirit Cats

Foudini, thought Great Dog, was a hopeless creature. It wasn't enough that they were swimming up to the island in full view. No, the cat had to make an announcement.

"Get the tablets ready!" shouted Foudini. "We'll show them the tablets right away!"

"Quiet!" said Steven.

"Amen!" said June.

They were coming up to the gray coast line. It was higher than they thought, and slippery. They felt Great Dog's feet touch ground, and then they were climbing onto the island. Before they had a chance to look around them, the mists swirled, thickened, and they were completely surrounded by spirit cats. "The tablets! The tablets!" Foudini called out. Great Dog stood up straight, so that they hung from his collar. In a loud voice, Foudini began reading the message of the tablets: "It is forbidden to don spirit suits," he read. "It is forbidden to attack the floating cities. We, the Egyptians, your masters, command you."

There was a sudden silence. The two Hoods, Foudini, and Great Dog waited for the spirit cats to fall before them as Foudini had said they would, to begin weeping because they had violated the sacred law, and to turn into small gray cats, running away from them as fast as their feet could carry them.

Instead, the backs of the cats rose up, and a long, high-pitched menacing wail broke from them. Behind them came two larger spirit cats carrying what looked like a banner with four words written on it.

"What does that say?" June asked, terrified.

"It says," Foudini answered, his voice trembling, "BEWARE OF FALSE PROPHETS!"

"What does that mean?" asked Steven.

"It means," said June, "that they're going to attack us."

"We didn't fool them?" Foudini asked, but no one had time to answer him. The spirit cats were moving toward them, leaping through the air. "Great Dog!" Foudini cried out. "Save me!" But Great Dog was fighting off the cats around him. They were much stronger than they had been when he last encountered them, and they were attacking, claws out and hissing. Great Dog fought ferociously because he wanted to free himself, and then free June, Steven, and the cat. Steven, who was surrounded by cats, had his head down and was charging into the side of the cat nearest him. June was running back and forth beneath Great Dog's belly, kicking at the spirit cats who came near her and jumping away from their claws. Foudini looked up and saw Great Dog, his ears flat against his head, his lips pulled back over his teeth, snarling. He had never realized how frightening Great Dog's teeth were, not even when he'd ridden in his mouth.

Great Dog was slowly clearing an area around him. Some of the spirit cats were retreating, limping and bleeding. The others, however, had formed a group and were whispering together. Great Dog picked Steven and June up in his mouth, told Foudini to jump on his back, and galloped to the island's edge.

"We're giving up?" Steven asked. "I can't believe we're giving up."

Great Dog was again swimming in the water. "Look up," he commanded. The round bubble of the city Steven had visited once before was slowly floating down through the gray mists. "My city," said Great Dog. "When the ladder comes down, everyone goes up."

"Thank heavens," said June.

"Thank heavens," said Foudini.

"I'm not going," Steven told Great Dog. "I'm staying with you."

A thick golden ladder was winding down through the air toward them. Foudini jumped from Great Dog's back high into the air and caught onto the ladder with his front paws. "Come *on*," he said, looking back. "We're safe here."

"This was all your idea," June reminded the cat, climbing onto the ladder behind him.

"The brave know when to run," Foudini said huffily. "Where do you think *you're* going?" he asked Great Dog, who, with Steven on his back, was beginning to swim off toward the island. "You're going *back*?" the cat shrieked in disbelief. "You can't go back without *me*. I'm the only one who knows what to do." Then the cat saw the floating city beginning to rise again. "How will we find you?" he cried out frantically.

"I'll find *you*," said Great Dog. And then he and Steven swam out of sight.

"What are we going to do?" asked Steven. "We can't fight all of them."

"Not the way we are now," said Great Dog, who seemed to be heading out to sea.

"Where *are* you going?"

"To the other side of the island," said Great Dog. "Where they don't expect to find us."

"But why?" asked Steven.

"You're going back?" the cat shrieked in disbelief.

"You'll see," said Great Dog.

"I'm not in the mood for surprises," Steven said. Great Dog, however, was already climbing up on the island shore and didn't answer him.

"Be quiet," Great Dog said. He sniffed the air. "I can breathe again! That means I can find it!"

"Find what?" asked Steven. "Find what?"

Great Dog was sniffing the ground and began trotting in circles. Then he began loping to the left. He stopped, sniffed again, went back, and ran off to the right. This time he didn't stop. "Here it is!" he said excitedly.

"Here what is?" Steven demanded.

"Hold on tight," said Great Dog.

In front of them, a spirit cat bounded into the air. Great Dog also leaped up and as he fell to the ground, he brought his front paws down on the back of the spirit cat. The cat wailed and pleaded to be let loose. Great Dog picked up the spirit cat and shook it until a small gray cat flew loose from its costume of mist and fog. "You'll stay in my mouth until this is over," Great Dog told the cat, "or I'll swallow you whole."

"What's going on?" asked Steven. "What are we doing?"

"This is the place," said Great Dog. "This is where they keep their spirit costumes."

"So?" said Steven.

"So we're going to put them on," said Great Dog.

The cat had been protecting a cave, and they went into it. There on the gray, damp walls were the costumes, one after another, as far back as the eye could see. Great Dog was putting one on.

"It will never fit you," said Steven, but the costume seemed able to stretch forever. It was like air. It expanded easily, growing as large as the creature that wore it.

"Put yours on," Great Dog told Steven. Steven began

struggling with it. "No, no," said Great Dog. "You've got it upside down. Put your front paws in the other way."

"Feet," said Steven. "Not paws."

"Feet, paws," said Great Dog. "Hurry up."

"It's cold in these things," said Steven. "But I feel *strong*."

"You *are* strong," said Great Dog. "These suits have powers."

"Now what?" asked Steven.

"Now we look for the other cats," said Great Dog. "And this little cat in my mouth is going to tell them that we *are* the true prophets."

"I won't," said the little cat, whose voice echoed inside Great Dog's mouth.

Great Dog began to growl. "Don't swallow me!" cried the little cat.

"Will you tell them?" asked Great Dog.

"I'll tell them!" said the little cat. "I'll do anything!"

"I'll tell you what to say," said Great Dog. "Can you remember all of that?" he asked when he was finished.

"I remember! I remember!" said the little cat.

"Let's go," said Steven.

"We don't have to go anywhere," said Great Dog. "Just look around you." The spirit cats had surrounded them. As Steven looked, he felt the air grow colder and damper. The air was gray and foggy and the cats were gray and misty. Grouped together as they were, they seemed to be ghosts, materializing and dissolving. Steven began shaking with cold and fear. From deep inside his spirit costume, Great Dog growled.

"We are the true prophets," said the small cat inside Great Dog's mouth. "You will be punished. We will take back your spirit-cat suits and from now on you will be ordinary cats. You have attacked the floating cities and ignored the prophets who came with our tablets. Bow down!"

The silence was absolute. The spirit cats seemed to have turned to stone. They watched Great Dog and Steven through narrow, slitted, icy eyes. Then, from deep inside his suit, Great Dog began howling. At that, the spirit cats threw themselves down on the ground, sobbing.

"They *are* the true prophets!" cried the biggest of the cats, who was evidently their leader. "They come with the bodies and words of cats, and the howling of dogs!"

"You must obey us," said the little cat in Great Dog's mouth. "You must give us the tablets with the spells for making the spirit-cat costumes."

Now the spirit cats began weeping. They looked toward their leader. "We must do what he says," said the huge spirit cat, retracting his claws.

He and two other cats disappeared into a tunnel and reappeared with seven rolls of papyrus. They laid the scrolls at the feet of Great Dog and Steven. Great Dog picked them up, tore them to shreds, and ate them. Inside his mouth, the little cat crouched beneath Great Dog's tongue to avoid being swallowed.

"Now you must give us your spirit-cat suits," said the little cat.

As Great Dog and Steven watched, the spirit cats seemed to shrink and melt, until finally only a crowd of little gray cats was left, standing in what looked like a cloud bank.

"We will take these," said the little cat, as Great Dog gathered up the costumes. "You must bring the other costumes from the caves."

Sadly, the little gray cats went into the cave and brought the spirit costumes out with them. Great Dog gathered them up in his teeth.

"Now we will take our leave of you," said the little cat. "Repent of your sins!" The little gray cats lay on their stomachs, stretching their front paws out toward Great

Dog and Steven. "We will be back," said the little cat, still in Great Dog's mouth, and then Great Dog and Steven bounded off through the mist, to the edge of the island, and into the water.

"We can *swim* in these," said Steven. "Much better than we could without them."

"Let me *out*," cried the little cat, who was hanging onto one of Great Dog's sharp, pointed teeth.

"I will," said Great Dog.

"Not *here*," said the little cat, "not in the middle of the ocean."

"I'll let you out soon enough," said Great Dog. "As soon as my city comes back for us."

"Not the city of dogs!" said the little cat.

"You'll like it there," said Great Dog. "Many of the dogs keep cats for pets. You'll be very happy. You'll see."

"Oh, woe!" said the little cat. "Oh, misery. Oh, dreadful fate!"

"Oh, shut up!" said Steven.

Above them, a great globe hovered, a huge bubble that began sinking slowly through the air toward them.

"Is that it?" asked the cat.

"That's it," said Great Dog.

He and Steven climbed the ladder. A crowd of happy dogs was waiting for them, tails wagging. Great Dog bounded over to his mother who licked his nose, lowered her head, and let June and Foudini, who were riding on her back, slide to the ground.

"What have you been doing?" Great Dog asked Foudini and June.

"Oh," said Foudini. "We've been having the most *wonderful* time. They've been having party after party for me. I'm their hero. They say that again and again. I'm the one whose tail poked a hole in the city wall when the two globes collided. Everyone says they'll never forget me. The dogs tell stories about me. I alone had the wisdom to know the wall of *this* city had to be punctured. I never knew dogs were such wonderful people! I want to stay here forever!"

"Good," said Great Dog gloomily.

"Why does your mouth seem full of fog?" Great Dog's mother asked him.

"Some outfits of the spirit cats," said Great Dog. "They're very useful. They make you stronger and when you wear them, you look terrifying."

"You have the suits?" asked Foudini. "How did you do *that*?"

"Some other time," said Great Dog. "I'll just listen to the stories and songs everyone's singing about you."

"Nonsense," said Great Dog's mother. "*I* want to hear how you got those things."

"Oh, fine," said Foudini. "The least little thing and everyone pays attention to that Great Oaf."

"He'll never change," said Steven.

"No, he won't," June agreed.

"Let's go have some lunch," said Great Dog's mother. Oh, no, thought Steven, remembering the dried liver.

"Where's the little spirit cat?" asked Great Dog. "He's staying here too. He'll make someone a wonderful pet."

"I don't see what's so wonderful about him," Foudini said.

Chapter 13

Going Home

Steven and June, Great Dog and Foudini were reading in the barn when Steven looked up and said the four of them had had some wonderful adventures together. Great Dog was startled. It was as if Steven now thought that their trips to the city of cats and the city of dogs had taken place long ago. He began to think about the time he had spent with the four Hoods. Next year, Steven would be going to college. In two years, June would be going, too. Life would not be the same. Suddenly and for the first time, he wanted to return to his own city and his own home. He looked at Foudini, innocently licking a paw, and wondered if the cat was ever homesick. He decided to wait until Steven and June had gone to bed before he asked him.

"Homesick?" said Foudini. "Never. I never think of home. The Hoods couldn't manage without me."

But Great Dog thought that the Hoods needed him less and less and, moreover, had less and less time for him. When Steven talked about the ski trip the seniors were taking at the end of the month, the dog became even more miserable. Soon Steven would be gone, and Great Dog could not follow him. In this world, Great Dog thought, he was too big to go anywhere.

"But don't you want to go back to your own world?" Great Dog persisted. "Sometimes?"

"I'm too important here," said Foudini.

"Fine, fine," said Great Dog. "Let's not talk about it."

"You'll see," said the cat.

Great Dog watched sadly as Steven made his preparations to leave on the ski trip. He watched sadly as Steven got on the bus, carrying his skis. He wasn't needed. He would tell Steven how he felt when he came back from his trip. Then Great Dog felt restless and decided to go over the tops of the mountains and watch Steven skiing. He would go in the morning, when the light was best.

Great Dog went to sleep unaware that Steven and the others who had gone on the trip were trapped in a snowslide, unable to dig themselves out. And while Great Dog slept, an icy rain fell, which froze and turned the mountainside on which they were trapped into ice.

The next morning, Great Dog arrived, planning to spy on Steven. Instead, he heard the children crying and saw them trying to dig themselves out. He began to climb toward them, but the ice was slippery and his long nails could not dig in. Again and again, he slid backward. Finally, he stood helplessly at the foot of the cliff. "Woof!" he called in his great voice. "Woof! Woof!"

"Great Dog!" the children cried. "Now we'll be safe!"

But the dog could not reach them, and when he did not reach them, the children began to lose hope. They felt colder and ever more hopeless.

Great Dog turned around and galloped back to the four Hoods. He picked up Mr. Hood's scent and tracked him to a house whose roof he was repairing. When his barking only caused Mr. Hood to mutter angrily at him, he plucked Mr. Hood from his ladder and galloped off with him until they were at the foot of the mountain. Mr. Hood stopped shouting and waving his arms. He looked at the mountain, and he looked at Great Dog, and he told Great Dog to take him back to town and to the fire department.

The fire marshall called men who came in helicopters. Great Dog sat with Mr. and Mrs. Hood and watched as the men were lowered down onto the mountain, dug footholds for themselves, and began digging the children out. Soon Steven was lifted into the helicopter and in a few minutes, he was back with Mr. and Mrs. Hood.

Great Dog watched all this and concluded that it was indeed true: he was no longer needed. He would stay, however, until Steven and June went to college.

"Some day," he told Steven, "I might want to go back to The Other Side. You know you can always find me if I go. On that side, I'll live forever. If you want me, just come to the place on top of the mountain and put a note through to my side."

"Some day," said Steven. "But not *soon.*"

"Not soon," said Great Dog, who felt as if he had already left.

But two years passed as if they were only days, and June was soon to go to college. Once she was gone, Great Dog lay down with Foudini. "I think I'll just go home for a short visit," he said.

"You're not fooling me," said the cat. "You'll never come back."

"I might," said Great Dog.

"How can you bear to leave *me?*" asked Foudini.

"Sooner or later," said Great Dog, "I'll see you on The Other Side."

"Nonsense," said Foudini. "The four Hoods will always have *me.* They always say they don't know what they'd do without *me.* When are *you* thinking of going?"

"Ummm," said Great Dog. "Now." And he got up, left the barn, and made his way up the mountain, found where the horizon ended and grew solid, peeled the sky from the wall, and went through. "Of course I'll be back," he said as he began to pick up the pieces of the sky and put them back. "One day I'll be back."

Without Great Dog, Foudini found himself lonely. He lived for school vacations, when June and Steven came home, brought him new books, let him use their typewriters, and recited the stories of his adventures, which were the stories he liked hearing best. But he was beginning to feel old, and he knew that on The Other Side he would not age and would be safe. He thought he had used up seven of his nine lives in this world, and it was, perhaps, time to return to The Other Side. Once there, he would find a way to visit Great Dog. He decided to return to The Other Side when June and Steven returned to college.

The children left, and still Foudini put off leaving the barn. Then Mrs. Hood decided the time had come for him to go to the veterinarian's for his shots, and Foudini decided it was time to leave. As the pickup truck turned the corner to the vet's, Foudini jumped down, found the building behind which a small part of the sky was always dark, peeled the strips of darkness away, saw the mist and the cat tails on the other side, and walked slowly through. He could feel the gray island of his childhood approaching. "I'll be back soon," he said through the crack. He picked up the strips of darkness and placed them carefully over the crack. The children, he thought, will be lonely, but not for long. They will forget us.

The island was a few inches from the shore. He jumped and was on it. In a few minutes, he would find the entrance to the tunnels and soon would be home with his mother. Dried fish and dried fish heads! He didn't know why he was crying.

The four Hoods were standing side by side, looking at their house in the country. "It looks like the experiment succeeded," said Mr. Hood. "We're still here."

"But now," said Steven, "we're *only* the four Hoods. We're not the four Hoods and Great Dog."

"The four Hoods, Great Dog, *and* Foudini," June corrected.

"No, we're just us," said Steven.

"But they'll be back," said June. "I know they will."

"They will," Mr. Hood agreed.

"They haven't really *gone* anywhere," said Mrs. Hood. "At least *I* feel as if they're still here."

"Watching us," said Mr. Hood.

Steven and June looked at one another. They were suddenly absolutely sure it was true. Somewhere Great Dog and Foudini were watching them.

"Let's go in," Steven said to June. "I want to read some stories."

"Stories?"

"The ones we wrote about the school bus and the spirit cats. Those stories. We'll read them while we wait for them to come back."

Mr. and Mrs. Hood looked at one another and shook their heads. "They have to believe they'll come back," said Mr. Hood. "They're lonely."

Mrs. Hood said she expected they *would* come back. She was sure of it. Mr. Hood put his arm around her and hugged her. It was odd, he said, not to have that dinosaur around, falling through the roof, or that strange cat, sitting on the floor, turning the pages of his book.

On his island, Foudini heard that and smiled. Great Dog, who was visiting the cat, rumbled contentedly and wagged his tail. He knew that sooner or later, Steven or June would go up the mountain, slip a note through the crack in the sky, and they would once again be together.